Legacy of the Succubus

Kim Bair

Facebook: kimbairauthor
Instagram: KimBairAuthor
Email: kimbair@proton.me
Website: www.kimbair.com
Telegram: kimbairauthor

More books by Kim Bair:
Dead Shifter Walking, The Succubus Executioner Book 1
Demigod Down, The Succubus Executioner Book 2
A Witch's Fury, The Succubus Executioner Book 3
A Council of Betrayal, The Succubus Executioner Book 4
Death of a Succubus, The Succubus Executioner Book 5
Legacy of the Succubus, The Succubus Executioner Book 6
Creation of the Dual Shifter, The Dual Shifter Executioner
The Mel Files
Andy's Origin, The Andromalius Chronicles

Chapter 1

Eventually, Tommy and I made our way down from the roof of Halfling. I paused, watching him walk back among the few remaining guests at Grams's wake. Or funeral, or whatever the fuck word appropriately conveyed that she was dead and gone forever. My heart constricted painfully, my gaze sweeping the interior of the nightclub turned funeral parlor, or ... whatever.

Kass had done a good job with the place—solid wood tables and chairs, new lighting, and an updated sound system. My gaze landed on Logan's wide back, his black jacket stretched taut. I didn't recognize who he was speaking to. I debated a moment, unsure if I wanted to sink into his embrace or drink. Alcohol won.

The bartender finished wiping down a glass and looked up at me. "What can I get ya?"

"Something strong," I requested, leaning against the wood, tilting my body to watch Logan. He felt it. I knew it.

My head throbbed lightly and I checked my shields, finding them weakening. Rubbing my temple and grinding my jaw, I willed them to stay in place.

"Stop forcing it," Anna advised as she plopped herself next to me, her fire red hair cut short in an adorable bob. Deadly, but adorable. Her blue eyes slid over to the bartender.

"I'll have what she's having," she demanded.

"A please wouldn't hurt," I reminded her, massaging my temple again.

She turned her icy blue stare at me, raising one crimson eyebrow. I responded with my own intense, sea green gaze. With a huff that fluffed her bangs, she turned back to the bartender, who was watching our exchange with interest as he worked.

"Pleeeeease," she drew out the word, her inflection making it sound insulting.

He didn't acknowledge her, setting our drinks down on pristine white napkins.

"Thanks," I muttered, before taking a large gulp.

Anna sat on the leather padded stool, never ceasing to survey the room with her gaze, ankles crossed in her black dress.

"Is that my dress?" I asked, pulling at the sleeve.

She shrugged, "I didn't pack for a funeral."

I grunted a response, turning away from her and pulling my drink closer. The cool liquid between my palms helped take my mind off the growing throbbing in my temples.

"Stop forcing it," Anna repeated, slowly and clearly. I glared at her.

"I don't have time to build them up slowly. Nor do I have the desire to influence those around us." Being shot and almost dying had destroyed my guards. Guards I needed to survive and blend into society. Otherwise, everyone within a mile would be at the mercy of my volatile emotions.

As succubi, our greatest strength rested in our ability to push and pull emotions. Granted, Anna and I were only half succubus, we now knew; we had previously thought we were pureblood lab creations of the late and demented Selena.

Our mother was the ruling Queen Bitch of the red hell our people had been shoved into lifetimes ago by the once powerful witches.

My father and Anna's traded us to Selena.

"Whatever you are thinking about is seriously pissing you off," Anna commented, taking a sip.

I groaned, putting the cool glass to my lips and finishing off the contents. I set the glass down with a loud click before turning to her and throwing my shields up again, the throbbing in my head doubling.

Cracking my neck, I asked, "Better?"

She shrugged, sipping her drink daintily.

"So, I've been thinking about my living situation," she began, cradling her drink between her hands as she looked over at me.

I was tempted to tell her this was hardly the time, but I needed the distraction. I could feel Logan probing at me and I was tempted to shield myself from him. He didn't need my misery and pain, but I lacked the strength.

I hoped he wasn't picking up on that. We had been doing so well lately. Even though our mating wasn't planned or discussed, I secretly liked the fact that he was stuck with me forever. I knew I wasn't an easy person to deal with. Having the security of the mate mark, or in my case two mate marks, put me at ease.

2

Which meant I probably should have felt bad for Logan.

"Yeah, you should start paying rent," I told her, signaling the bartender for another drink.

She huffed at me, "You must be joking."

"Running the mansion and keeping the kids clothed and fed isn't cheap. Besides, what about your law practice in New York?"

She shrugged. "I may just leave it. I certainly wasn't a partner. My cases have already been reassigned."

I probed her nonchalant attitude, wondering why the sudden change. I had expected her to hightail it from town as soon as I was vertical.

"You want to be part of this circus now?" I asked. She hadn't when we escaped from Selena. The only thing she'd wanted then was a normal life. The chance to forget about the hell we had endured at Selena's hands. I couldn't blame her, but I also couldn't change who and what I was.

"The Oracle," she began, rolling the glass between her hands. "She might have made a few solid points about me."

I said nothing, accepting my refill from the bartender and taking a large belt, rolling the amber liquid about my mouth.

I felt her waiting on me, but I didn't have much to say to that. The Oracle, while annoying with her games, was direct in her observations. Whatever she'd said to Anna had hit home.

"You could always pick up cases to make rent," I suggested.

She turned to me, surprise evident in her face. Unlike me, she wasn't broadcasting her emotions. I took her advice and let my guards down slightly, feeling the throbbing in my temples ease. I mirrored Anna's position, my hands cradling the drink as we leaned against the bar.

"How many cases?" Anna asked.

I shrugged. "Depends on how long each case takes you. Although I'll warn you, don't try to mooch off me. I will evict you."

She chuckled, raising her glass in a toast. "To hell and back, and same Olivia."

"Some things never change," I agreed.

Anna turned as Logan crossed the distance between us. "And some things do," she whispered softly.

Logan raised a caramel eyebrow, his black jacket stretched across broad shoulders and down to a tapered waist. He wrapped his arm around my shoulders, pulling me into his shifter warmth.

"You doing okay?" he asked softly against my ear.

I nodded. "Anna was just brainstorming jobs she can pick up."

I felt Logan's annoyance through the mate bond.

"You are staying?" he asked her.

"Yep," the word was clipped from her and I shook my head. I needed to ask what had happened between them.

Logan grunted, sparing her a long and pointed look before turning to me. "Are you ready to go?"

I nodded, finishing my drink.

"Don't worry, I'll find my own ride home," Anna called out to us.

"I wasn't," I answered.

"The kids?" I asked softly as we exited into the dying light of the evening.

"Hudson took them home," Logan stated, unlocking the SUV.

I grunted, seeing my own SUV parked in the lot as well. Frickin' Anna.

I slipped into the passenger seat with an annoyed huff.

"Do you want to talk about what's going on between you and Anna?" I asked.

Logan sighed, sparing me a glance as he backed up the vehicle.

"I don't like her."

"I picked up on that."

He gave me a half smile. "She showed up while I was out of town, was difficult with Tommy, ordered everyone around, got you kidnapped, and wouldn't check on Darren. Do I need additional reasons?" he asked me.

I turned, looking out the window and mulling it over. "I'd like for you two to get along. She's a vital part of my past and you are my future."

Logan said nothing so I continued on, "But I suppose I understand. If the situation was reversed, I'd have a hard time accepting her, too."

After all, I still had reservations about Hudson, Logan's cousin. He'd better hope he didn't step out of line in front of me. I wasn't above killing him for doing a piss poor job as the Western Compass Alpha and letting a rebellion shoot me.

Logan had taken care of everything while my soul was gallivanting on a scavenger hunt in the strange, red-laden dimension of the succubi. I drummed my fingers on the center console, my mind slowly turning back to business.

"What do you think will happen to Kitten?" I asked.

He shrugged, resting his large, warm palm over my own to still my fingers.

"Grams made Hash her beneficiary for all her assets," Logan reminded me.

"What if she was bluffing?" I questioned.

Logan shifted in the driver's seat, turning to gauge my interest in the matter. "You've never been concerned with Kitten before."

"Green light," I informed him.

A smile grew on his face, until I raised an eyebrow and pointed out the windshield. He grunted, turning his attention back to the road.

It was my turn to shift uneasily. "That was before. When Grams still had control of it, I don't know, it felt right, natural. I don't want someone I don't know running the club."

Logan nodded silently, finally saying, "I don't know if Grams's attorney will release that information to us."

But his silent communication was far stronger: Let it go.

I should have. It was just a brick-and-mortar building. I could make another one, hell I could build twenty, but sentimentality had me wanting the original. I knew Hash had a wife. How could she possibly plan on managing a club full of succubi?

I could make them all quit, but that seemed petty. Even for me.

The rest of the drive back was uneventful. It was still early by our standards, and while I wanted to lie in bed and forget everything, there were several unresolved issues that would have followed me there.

"I thought I'd find you in here," I said to my father's hunched form in the library.

"Tommy attempted to teach me how to look on-line," he said, forming the word with distaste, "but I find the simplest of forms the best."

I nodded, sitting across from him at my favorite writing desk. We had found it at an estate auction; Logan was certain it was haunted. The intricately carved legs alone were a labor of love, the thick top refinished to a perfect shine. Plus, there was a lion crest carved into the chair. It was meant to be ours.

"How was your funeral?" He asked the question offhandedly, but I felt his interest. I was hopeful it was in my well-being.

I shrugged, picking lint off my black dress, not wanting to meet his gaze, not wanting to show the weakness of my tear-stained eyes. "It's done," I forced, my voice betraying my ragged emotions.

I lifted my gaze to find him studying me. I stared into eyes a perfect color match for my own.

"Your guards are better," he kindly changed the subject.

I rubbed my temple. "It's taking a lot out of me."

He nodded, watching me closely. "It didn't before?"

I shook my head.

"Are there any other changes you have noticed?" he asked.

I shrugged. "The mate bond has changed. Before, I had access to everyone's thoughts. Now I only can communicate with Logan silently."

My father nodded, closing the leather-bound book with a long sigh, drumming his fingers on it.

"Not finding what you needed?" I questioned, hopelessness welling inside of me.

"No." He drummed his fingers faster, thinking. "I need the books from my library."

I nodded, dropping my arms into my lap and resting my back against the chair. I was trying not to cross my arms over my chest, trying not to take a defensive position for what I knew was coming.

"I don't have things in order for the mermaids. I do have a lead on the land for the unicorns, but it's not where we originally agreed," I treaded carefully.

He rubbed his forehead, leaning back in his own chair.

"He hasn't recovered yet," announced Doyle the minotaur, stomping on cloven feet in the same green tunic and trimmed brown leather he'd been wearing since we met. I looked over his salt and pepper fur, wondering if he bathed.

"Doyle, do you want other clothing?" I asked. I had largely ignored both of them to deal with the attack of the rogues and Grams's death.

I looked at my father, still dressed in his clothing from the red world. "Both of you?" I amended.

"Where do you suppose we'll find clothing for a minotaur?" my father asked. "Even in our world, that was a challenge."

I shrugged, "I can find a seamstress who can make him whatever he wants."

"Will I have to be hidden?" Disgust was laced heavily around that last word.

"You don't like the cloaking spells?" I asked.

Doyle shook his black and silver head.

I almost told him too fucking bad, I don't have time to handle your identity issues along with everything else. But I stopped myself, rubbing a finger against my bottom lip.

"You certainly don't have to be cloaked for the clothing, but going out in public is bound to cause issues."

The library door pushed opened and they both turned. I knew Logan was approaching, feeling my angst at the situation.

"We should hold a press conference, Olie. It's the simplest way to deal with him being here, straight on. It also wouldn't hurt to address the humans now that things have settled down." Logan, always the problem solver.

I grunted, nodding. I didn't enjoy being in the public eye. We succubi still hadn't come out of the Supernatual closet quite yet. Truth be told, I wasn't sure I ever planned on it. There was safety in our silence and we fit into the human population easily.

The door opened again and this time Grant popped his head in.

"I'm sorry to do this now, Olie, but we've got a problem." His eyes were bloodshot. Grant and Ali now ruled the Supernatural Council in Grams's place. The three of them had been very close. I had thought Grant and Ali might walk when she left, but at the end of the day, Grams had sided with the late, Supe-hating Governor Hash. Ali and Grant were more exotic Supernaturals, like myself.

My father's chair and mine scraped in unison as we stood. "What's wrong?" I asked.

"The Vampire High Council is flying in and requests a meeting with you," Grant said, his eyes serious behind his glasses.

I grunted.

Logan looked and felt worried.

"They need to fix their damn mess," I said.

"Things are never that simple with the vampires," Logan warned. He was right, but damn if I was going to admit it out loud.

"Alright. Logan, schedule the press conference. Grant, schedule a meeting with the vampires. Magician, Doyle, I'll work on getting you both clothing."

"Uhh," Grant began.

"What?" I asked, a little too sharply.

"The vampires will only talk with you. I have them on hold in my office."

I laughed, shocked. "You put the High Council on hold?"

Even Logan chuckled.

"Alright, let's go, this is going to be priceless."

Logan, still in his black dress pants, walked next to me to Ali and Grant's office in the other wing of the house. We hadn't done much in the way of decorating, but the kids had put up random posters sporadically.

"Who is One Direction?" I asked, passing boys in bad need of a haircut.

"Some British group," Grant muttered. "Cindy is obsessed with them."

I nodded. "You should call Jerry," Logan offered. "I bet he would have an idea on who to call for clothing for Doyle."

I nodded, reluctant. "I had wanted to give them a little more time off."

Logan's heavy hand rested on my shoulder, pulling me close. I tucked into his warmth, breathing in his reassuring scent. "They want to help."

"I'll call once we get done with the vampires."

Grant pushed open a set of white doors into their office.

I sat behind his desk, the black chair still warm. Picking up the black phone, he hit a button before handing it to me.

"Olivia," I said into the receiver.

"Olivia, how wonderful of you to take my call. Please accept my deepest sympathies on such a tragic day."

I grunted, annoyed.

The silence stretched out. If he was expecting a thank you for calling on such a shitty day, he was barking up the wrong tree.

"What do you want?" I demanded.

"The High Council would like an audience."

"When and where?" I clipped out.

"We will send a vehicle for you."

"That's not how this—" The line went dead. "Mother fuckers," I hissed, looking at the receiver before slamming it back into the cradle.

I glared at Grant, and he stepped back. "Let security know, not one single vampire is allowed past the gate."

"What about Mal?" Logan asked.

"Not even Mal. These fuckers aren't playing anymore and I don't trust them."

Logan huffed, "The rogue army of Zachariah alone was evidence of that."

I turned my pointed glare at him and he raised an eyebrow. "Let's assume the Vamp Council knew about it. The question is: Are they here to do damage control or finish what Zachariah couldn't?"

Logan growled, "They would be fools to attempt anything."

"We are weak. I'm recovering from gunshot wounds, my father from magical crap, and our morale is low with the death of Grams. If I was going to take over the Supernatural Council, I couldn't imagine a better time."

Logan growled, having nothing to counter my points with.

I stood, pulling my phone out of my back pocket. "Let's focus on what we can control."

I dialed Jerry.

"Hey Olie, everything okay?" he answered, sleep lacing his voice heavily.

"Hey Jerry, I'm sorry to bother you, but I need some help."

"Yeah, anything."

"Do you know of a tailor who can make Doyle clothing, and do you want to take my dad shopping?"

This was such a small issue. I shouldn't be bothering him with it.

"Yeah, shopping is just what I need. I'll make a few calls on Doyle."

"Perfect. Let me know what you find." I was about to end the call but changed my mind. "Oh and Jerry, be careful of the vampires. The High Council is coming into town."

Jerry grunted, "Got it."

I stowed my phone in my back pocket again, turning to look at Logan. "Do you have Raphael's number?"

He nodded, pulling out his own phone. Grant continued to watch us in his office. It had to be awkward for him. I didn't care.

I listened to the ringing, staring at Logan's phone on speaker. My anger was spiking the longer we went without a response. Eventually, his voicemail picked up and Logan left a message, which was more than I would have done.

"Give him the benefit of the doubt. He did assist us with the rogues," Logan advised, feeling my short temper.

"It's all too fucking perfect, Logan. We granted him permission to set up a secondary House here. Not to mention all the new vampires we added to his damn line. We set him up as a powerhouse and now the fucking High Council is coming in."

"We don't know that," Logan tried again.

"I do know I'll kill the fucker if it turns out to be true. It's my damn turn to kill the asshole Master Vampires."

Logan grunted, a small smile tugging at the corner of his mouth. Okay, so I was a little sore about him killing both Tate and Zachariah. They might not have been the ones who shot me, but Zachariah did quite a number slicing and dicing on my unresponsive body.

"Has your father made any advances in freeing your power?" Logan asked.

I shook my head. "He needs the books back in the red world, but neither of us is strong enough for the trip."

Logan nodded. A boost of power certainly wouldn't have harmed anything at that point.

"We have other issues."

Logan and I turned as a unit to Grant.

"The human government is trying to re-form. They've been having issues since the lieutenant governor was also killed in the rogue attacks. They have been trying to agree on who takes over next. I believe they have agreed on a senator moving into the position temporarily until an emergency election can be held."

I waited. "And what does that have to do with us?"

Grant gave me a pained expression, but it was Logan who answered. "Grams was heavily involved with the human government. It would behoove us to be as well."

"Why?" I demanded.

He gave me an annoyed look. "Because unlike you, who have remained in the metaphorical closet, shifters have not. We need them to approve us as citizens with full rights."

"Oh, that hasn't been resolved yet?" He was right. I wasn't paying any damn attention.

"It has not."

"Great. So how do we get an invite to that mess?"

"We've been invited to a fundraiser for those injured in the rogue attacks. Senator Vargas will be there."

"I guess I need Jerry to go shopping for me as well," I grunted.

"When is this fundraiser?" Logan asked.

"Tomorrow night. Ali and I were going to attend, but..." He shook his head, rubbing his eyes when they teared up.

"You've been under a lot of pressure keeping everything running, Grant. We can handle it from here," I told him, feeling the sheer anxiety vibrating around him.

He nodded, blowing out a breath. "I just—I always thought she would come back, you know?"

"I know." I would be lying if I said that back in the far reaches of my heart I hadn't expected some sort of reconciliation with Grams. Her sudden death stole that from me. It was another reason I wanted to kill Zachariah.

There was nothing to be done about it now.

"Send the info to Logan's email. We will take care of it."

Grant nodded, drawing a breath, unable to look at us. Logan turned and I followed him out, closing the door softly behind us. Even with my subpar hearing compared to Logan's, I could hear Grant's sobbing. I couldn't fix it, not any of it, and I think that's what stung the worst.

There was no one to fight against. No mystery to unravel and fix, no wrong to right. Grams was dead and buried. So I was going to do what I usually did when my emotions were too much for me to handle, stay too damn busy to notice. Oh, and drink.

"No," Logan said.

I turned to him with a raised eyebrow. "Excuse me?"

"Whatever you are thinking that has you feeling so reckless, the answer is no, and stop blocking me."

I narrowed my eyes at him. "I didn't ask for permission, and I'm not trying to."

Logan sighed, turning to me before opening the door to our room.

"Can you just hold tight for now? Give us a few days of normalcy?"

"We don't have normal, Logan."

He rubbed his forehead. "You want to run."

He looked at me for denial. I wasn't going to lie to him. I set my chin.

"I won't stop you."

"You can't stop me."

He sat down heavily on the bed. "Stop it, Olie. I just got you back, don't put your guards up with me."

He held his arms out and I debated. Did I walk into them and fall apart into the million dejected pieces I was composed of? Or did I walk out and refuse to give in to my weakness?

Neither option sounded appealing. I sat next to him instead.

"Alright, I'll stay put."

"Thank you."

"But not because you asked, because there is shit else going on."

Logan laughed, pulling me into his warm embrace. "Whatever you need to tell yourself."

Chapter 2

It was an uneventful night. I didn't sleep much in bed, if at all. I ended up watching TV downstairs, in the company of Ginny's baby monitor and a huge bag of chips.

Around four in the morning Tommy sat down next to the chips. We didn't say anything. We didn't need to.

...

At some point I drifted off, waking up with Tommy's dark head on my shoulder. I blinked, looking at the early morning light filtering through the plantation shutters. A noise on the baby monitor had me carefully extracting myself from under Tommy. He settled on the couch without complaint.

Picking up the monitor, I saw Ginny sitting there, staring at the screen and waiting. I turned it off and set it back down on the end table before dragging myself up the stairs.

"Hey princess," I greeted her, softly opening her door. She instantly started babbling and pulling herself up on her crib.

Yawning widely, I picked her up, happy to cuddle her soft form against my chest for a few moments. I rocked her gently, her little arms pulled underneath her, her soft cheek resting against my chest.

Heaving a contented sigh, I looked down at her. "You smell."

She giggled.

...

Sitting the now cleaned and changed Ginny in her highchair, I knew Logan was up. Feeling me awake had probably roused him out of whatever crap sleep he was able to get.

Tommy oozed from sleeping on the couch to being wrapped in a throw at the farm table with his head down.

"Go to sleep," I told him.

"Don't wanna," he slurred.

"Whatever, you're big enough to make those decisions." He grunted his agreement, well I assume it was agreement.

Logan padded down the stairs, barefoot in black track pants and a white shirt. He rubbed at his eyes and I felt his exhaustion along the mate bond. With a sigh I turned back to the fridge, taking out sweet potatoes for Ginny.

"Hungry?" Logan grunted at me, pulling out eggs, butter, and cheese from the fridge.

I nodded, slipping to the microwave to warm up Ginny's food.

Logan worked silently at the stove and I smelled French toast as well, my favorite. I smiled at his back while trying to coax another bite into Ginny.

"Come on, missy girl, open big!" I said to her.

She slammed her hands on her white tray. "Mama!" her tiny voice yelled.

I froze, spoon held aloft. I wasn't her mother. Was she asking for Lorraine? Did she know the difference?

Logan leaned down, kissing her cheek. "Is that mama?" he asked, pointing at me.

"I'm not her mother," I told him. I regretted the words instantly, seeing the hurt in his eyes.

Tommy lifted his head up. "Olie, you feed her, take care of her, and change her dirty diapers. You're not biologically her mother, but in every other sense, you fulfill the role."

"Yeah, but I'm not her mother."

"Yes, you are," Logan said softly.

I turned at him, my emotional state highly unstable.

"What's a mother, Olie? Mine left me to suffer and die. Family is more than blood. You taught me that," Tommy continued on.

I nodded, understanding his point, but still uncomfortable with it.

"You made sure she lived, not once, but twice. You stopped Lorraine from poisoning her in the womb. You made the deal with Mal to heal her preemie body. I've felt the love you hold for her, Olivia. Why does her thinking you are her mother terrify you so?"

I wasn't good enough to be her mom. She was too perfect, too precious. She needed someone who could teach her how to love, how to be normal, and how not to be a raving psycho with a penchant for killing. All character traits I've never had.

How did I put that into words?

"Okay, I get it," Logan said softly, feeling my turbulent emotions along the mate bond. He leaned down, kissing my cheek before setting a plate of food in front of me.

"Mama!" Ginny demanded again.

I turned to her, blowing out a terrified breath before giving her another bite of sweet potatoes.

Logan set down a plate of food in front of Tommy, who looked up from his sitting position and grunted.

"Eat. If you are going to be a tired mess all day, at least be a fed mess," Logan commanded.

I laughed while Tommy glared at Logan's retreating back. He did take a bite, though. Not many defied the leader of the shifters.

Logan brought two plates loaded down with sausage, eggs, and his own French toast back to the table. I dropped a scrambled egg onto Ginny's tray. It immediately disappeared.

"She needs her veggies," Logan corrected me.

I rolled my eyes at him. "Right, because we are so great about consuming them." I looked pointedly at his plate before meeting his gaze.

"I will feed you spinach for breakfast," he threatened.

I laughed, "Just be glad it wasn't a donut, and that's just rude."

"Did you let Jerry know about needing a dress for tonight?" Logan asked.

I nodded. "Do you need clothing?" I asked him.

"No, I have a few outfits remaining from my before-Olivia collection."

"Before Olivia? What's that supposed to mean?" Tommy questioned.

"Before I had to shift or fight at every formal event we ever attend, hence ruining my clothing."

"Hey—" I was about to dispute the fact that I got into a fight at EVERY formal occasion, but I was having a hard time coming up with one where I hadn't.

Tommy must have picked up on that as he took his plate to the sink, laughing.

"Whatever, life has never been so interesting," I countered.

"That is also true," Tommy agreed, his eyes laughing. "That is also true."

"What's on the agenda until Jerry gets here?" Logan asked.

I shrugged, tossing Ginny more egg. "TV?" I suggested.

15

Logan nodded, taking his plates to the sink. "I can't say we've ever just hung out and watched TV."

...

Jerry arrived during a marathon binge on a crime show drama. Ginny was busy exploring what all the buttons of Tommy's laptop did. He had set her up with some baby program so she wouldn't break anything. At least, I hoped she didn't. I would end up paying for it.

I was tucked under Logan's arm, resting my eyes. I wasn't sleeping.

"Go see The Magician and Doyle first," Logan muttered.

"I'm awake," I slurred, sitting up and rubbing my eyes.

"Easy, baby girl, I already have your outfit ready. Let me go set up with the other two," Jerry said, an Asian woman trailing behind him.

I nodded, falling back into Logan's embrace.

It felt like only a few minutes before Logan's phone alarm was going off.

"What's that?" I slurred.

"Time to get ready," he answered.

I opened my eyes with a groan. "Jerry finish up?"

"He's taking your father shopping now."

I nodded, padding upstairs. "Where's Ginny?" I asked.

"Napping."

I pushed open the door to our room and padded to the shower. Logan followed behind me. "How much time do we have?"

"An hour," he answered, closing the door before heading to the closet. I wrapped my arms around him from behind. We had been celibate for too long. My body was healed, and my heart needed a hot and steamy distraction.

Logan turned in my embrace, his fingers gently trailing over my cheek. "We don't have to do this, Olivia."

"We do. I'm a soul-sucking succubus, remember?" I teased.

Logan laughed. I pushed away all the grief surrounding my heart, the guilt and uncertainty. I just wanted him and his love. I pushed up on my toes, my palms resting against his warm chest. Logan dropped his lips to my own, tentative at first.

I exhaled a contented sound, feeling him pressed against me, finding his mouth warm and welcoming. His strong hands cupped my face, controlling the

16

kiss with expert delicateness. A low growl issued from the back of this throat, his raw need flooding the mate bond.

My head tilted up, his thumbs running along my jaw line. Like a dam bursting, our pent-up desire flooded us both. His lips took advantage of the soft flesh of my neck, his greedy mouth biting down hard on my smaller mate mark. I bucked against him, heat and desire flooding my body. I growled as well, before pushing him back into our room and onto the bed.

...

I watched Jerry examining my wet hair in the bathroom mirror. "What are you thinking tonight?" he asked me, the question followed by laughter.

"Yeah, I have no idea why you asked me that, either," I confessed. Jerry had picked out a beautiful and classy navy blue dress with a wide V-neck and short cap sleeves. The natural waist fit perfectly and the extra bounce from the petticoat gave it a fun flair that contradicted my usual scowl.

"I still don't understand your hair color," Jerry muttered as he finished massaging product into my strawberry blond locks.

"I know, ever since I woke up it's been back to its natural color, no roots or anything," I answered him, looking at my reflection in the mirror and trying not to think about how similar my hair was to my mother's.

"We can change it," Jerry offered, picking up on my distress at realizing that I'd always kept this color hidden under layers of dyes.

"I know." I just wasn't sure I wanted to. It was also a reminder that I had a family. I wasn't lab created after all, and that gave me something primal back.

Jerry had matched Logan's suit perfectly to my dress. Logan stood in the pants and crisp white shirt, shoving a forkful of something in his mouth.

"What are you eating?" I asked, inhaling the scent of soy and spices.

"Chicken teriyaki with noodles," he answered, slurping a bite.

I scowled at him.

"There are veggie rolls downstairs," he defended as I continued to glare at him. He rolled his eyes. "And chicken-free lettuce wraps, deep fried orange cauliflower, and fried rice."

"That's better," I told him before the blow dryer ended our conversation.

Jerry worked silently and I watched him in the mirror. His face was drawn, his eyes focused, grief still etched on his features.

He finished blow drying and I was bored.

"Stop staring at me, Olivia."

I huffed. He smoothed down the soft curls he had skillfully crafted.

He met my gaze in the mirror.

"Yes, I miss her, but honestly, I feel guilty. Because I'm glad you are still here and that's what's most important to me," Jerry admitted.

I continued to look at him in the mirror. "There was a time I would have given my life for her," I admitted.

Jerry rested his hands on my shoulders.

"We need you, Olivia. No one else can lead us like you can."

I nodded at his reflection, refusing to cry and need to have my makeup reapplied. I wanted to believe him, but I knew I had crafted the Council from blood and fear. That was my legacy, and that's how I ruled. And never before had it bothered me, but I wasn't so sure anymore.

"I'm going to eat, thanks for the hair and makeup." I stood, rapidly blinking to dismiss the tears.

Jerry nodded, gathering up his supplies in silence.

Downstairs, Tommy was eyeballing my food. I sat down across from him, pulling a container with a fork sticking out to me. That Logan, always thoughtful.

"You know they are going to feed you at the fundraiser?" Tommy said.

"They have small portions and even smaller taste," I told him around a mouthful. "Here, have a veggie roll," I offered.

He gave me a look. "Ginny and I feel the same way about vegetables. Unless it's deep fried cauliflower, drowned in sugary orange sauce," he said, sneaking a bite from another open container. Where was he hiding that fork? And how much had he already eaten?

"Get your own!" I complained. He laughed, taking the container and fleeing the kitchen.

Logan took Tommy's place, watching him with a smile. I tried not to go all gooey at the open warmth on his face.

"The Magician and Doyle get settled?" I asked.

"Yes, your father and Jerry are going shopping after we leave. The tailor left with Doyle's measurements and the promise to make multiple options."

"That's good, he probably wants pants," I chuckled.

Logan shrugged, stealing my rice. I glared at him.

18

...

An hour later, we were making a tardy entrance to the fundraiser. Stepping out of the limo, I adjusted my dress.

"This looks familiar," I told Logan with a smile. Logan threaded our fingers together, pulling me closer to him.

"Does it?"

"Yeah, isn't this the place where I was your date when Lorraine was ill?" I asked him, ascending the steps.

He squinted at the building before looking down at me. "Is it?"

"I could be wrong, but I'm not."

Logan chuckled, "I suppose you are not."

We stopped at the open front door, a woman in a gold dress with a clipboard greeting us.

"Hello and welcome, can I get your invitation?" she asked politely.

Logan held out his phone. She read what was there, nodding before checking off our names on her clipboard.

"Please follow Roger, he will take you to your table."

Logan nodded and we followed behind the host to our assigned seats.

To my surprise, heads turned as we walked in, people's gazes following our progress.

"What are they saying?" I hissed to Logan, not enjoying our sudden popularity.

"They recognize you from the TV broadcast you hijacked."

"Oh." I had forgotten about that, what with mostly dying and rogue-mageddon and all.

Our host, Roger, pulled out my chair with a smile. I sat, trying to be dainty but failing miserably as I shuffled closer to the table.

Logan seated himself just fine. Asshole.

The woman to my left, set her reading glasses down, turned to introduce herself. "Hello dear, I'm Gretchen."

I smiled, taking her outstretched hand. "Olivia."

She nodded. "Wonderful venue, isn't it? I hear the shifters had their own soirée here."

I stifled my laugh and smiled out, "How fascinating." Apparently, Logan was going to keep some sort of anonymity.

"Aren't you the one that warned everyone about the attacking vampires?" Getchen continued on.

"I am." I probably should have corrected her use of the word vampire, but given my previous conversation with the spineless jackasses of their Council, I wasn't in the mood to help their PR campaign.

"Blasted beasts, they should all be put down."

"I'll drink to that," Logan muttered.

"They certainly have been causing their fair share of problems," I agreed. Surveying the scene, I commented, "I'm surprised we didn't miss the speakers."

"Senator Vargas had a few security issues to address, since the leader of the shifters is supposed to be here. I hear they are using silver bullets," she whispered to me.

I grunted, turning to look at Logan. His jaw tightened. I had silver hiding along my thighs, but my outfit didn't leave room to hide much else.

"Are they expecting a fight?" I asked, taking a sip of the champagne set in front of me.

Gretchen shrugged, "With those monsters, who can really tell?"

I opened my mouth to tell her what I thought about those monsters, but Logan squeezed my leg. I turned to him and he nodded toward the stage.

The woman in the gold dress from the door was now up there, waiting for everyone's rapt attention.

Gretchen was lucky. I swallowed down my biting words.

The woman up front put on a winning smile. "Thank you for coming out tonight." She paused for the applause. "And thank you for your support for Senator Vargas." More applause. I rested my chin in my palm with a long-winded sigh.

"I hate this crap," I hissed to Logan.

He took a drink from his own glass. "I know, but this is our best shot at speaking with the new Governor or acting Governor."

I shrugged.

The woman in gold droned on about how wonderful Senator Vargas was, how giving, how amazing, how perfect in judgment. Blah, blah, blah. I tried playing footsie with Logan under the table, but apparently our earlier romp had left him satisfied, or at least able to exercise better judgment than my own.

Gretchen clapped at each painful pause in the speech.

"With that, it is my pleasure to introduce Senator Hector Vargas." People actually stood up to clap, for a human who made rules. Logan glared at me from his elevated position, until I did the same with a scowl.

Senator Vargas took the stage, standing behind the wooden podium and waiting for the overzealous applause to die down. I sat down quickly with a huff of annoyance that wasn't unnoticed by Vargas. Can't say I gave a shit.

He's staring directly at us, I thought to Logan.

He is, he answered. Neither of us broke the stare-down until Vargas turned his attention to the room full of people who actually wanted it.

He smiled, and unlike Hash, there was some warmth behind it. His Mexican heritage was evident from his bronze skin, black hair, and matching dark brown eyes.

"Thank you, thank you," he began. "I am honored to be standing in front of you as the hopeful next Governor of our wonderful state. More fucking applause.

I groaned, they hadn't even fed us yet.

After droning on and on and on, Vargas finally shut up.

"Thank you all again for coming. Please enjoy the wonderful meal that has been prepared." People stood to cheer him off the stage. I hid a yawn; nothing he had said even stirred a response in me. I suppose it was also fair to note, however, that he hadn't mentioned us Supernaturals at all.

Interesting, considering I was fairly certain he knew we were here.

Waiters bustled about refilling drinks, dropping off bread, butter and salad.

I looked down at the leafy vegetables with a groan.

Logan laughed, "It may be the only thing you can eat." My stomach picked that moment to growl.

I sighed, picking up my fork and trying to find a section heavily laden with dressing.

Logan's prediction was correct, and it annoyed me. He enjoyed eating double portions of the small steaks they had provided along with the bacon potatoes.

"The asparagus is game," he said with a knowing laugh.

"I've eaten enough green shit for today, thanks."

Logan nodded, turning to face me, his gaze watching Vargas intently. "He should be making the rounds soon."

I nodded, surveying the room behind him. People were getting up from their seats, mingling. It appeared from their relaxed body language that no one expected trouble. Interesting. I was never calm whenever there was a gathering of Supernaturals. Especially when Logan or I was in the spotlight. But I suppose no one was likely to challenge Vargas for his tentative position and rightfully claim it by his death.

I huffed. Apparently, the events of the past few days were drawing out long forgotten-about memories. I settled my chin in my hand, thinking back on when I had challenged Hadrian for the Council...

"I've come for your head." I pointed my sword at Hadrian as he lounged on his golden throne.

The vampire beast smiled, fangs elongated, eyes ambered, drawing his long legs under him.

"Don't be foolish, little girl," he hissed at me, leaning forward, his silk shirt revealing hard white chiseled flesh.

Hadrian lived in a mansion he had swindled from one of his pets. A three-tiered inky chandelier cast light from cream candles, glittering against the teardrop crystals before casting eerie shadows below. The vampires didn't need the extra light. I'd have liked more illumination, but it wasn't my main priority.

Killing Hadrian and taking his seat at the head of the Council was.

"I told you to leave me alone," I reminded him.

He shrugged, leaning back against the inky throne with ruby jewels.

"It was just a siren. Why do you care if I drained her?" he asked.

I lowered my sword. "She was mine." I'd needed her alive to secure the trade I had arranged. His meddling had cost me a hefty sum.

He shrugged, a smile playing over his lips. "Not anymore."

I growled. "Get down here, Hadrian, your head is mine."

Hadrian came down from his throne one leisurely step at a time. "Come, pet, be one of my own. Do what I tell you, when I tell you. You don't want the headache of the Council."

I grunted, "I don't take orders well. I want your fucking head."

"Then I accept your challenge," Hadrian smiled, his dark eyes glittering.

I twisted my wrist, swinging my sword, watching him closely.

"Oh pretty, that weapon is useless against me," he chided.

"Guess we will see," I taunted.

In the eight months since I had freed myself from the insanity of Selena, I had learned that vampires were still assholes, humans were essentially worthless, and my succubus and incubus brethren were considered the lowest of the low in the Supernatural world.

It was a situation I was working on rectifying by killing one fucking asshole at a time. But I needed funds, and the siren deal was supposed to set me up for months.

"Do try not to ruin the silk, it's my favorite."

Hadrian kept his arms lose at his sides, sauntering as we began circling each other. I wasn't surprised. Everyone had underestimated me thus far, and this pathetic excuse for a Master Vampire was no different.

He faked a lunge at me, smiling.

I didn't flinch. He pulled back, laughing, and his entourage joined in, their naked bodies draped around his throne.

I'd had enough of his games. He turned, bowing before his horde of followers. I made my move, swiping my blade against his back, slicing deeply into his spine before cutting up and into his muscles.

He arched back, a scream of outrage and shock leaving his mouth. He turned back to me, anger contorting his features.

"How dare you!"

It was my turn to laugh. "I dared, whatcha gonna do about it?"

Hadrian lunged again, this time with no intent of faking me out. Arms outstretched, he tried to pin me against his body. His fighting technique was laughable. I twisted away easily, raising my sword once I had the distance. It cleaved up his side, leaving a beautiful trail of dark blood. He came at me again, not pausing in his attack, finally taking me seriously.

Good, I was bored.

His clawed nails tried to catch me, wanting to tear into my exposed flesh. I met him hit for hit and he never landed a claw. I scored numerous slices into his hands and forearms. It succeeded in pissing him off further.

I smiled, waiting for an opening, biding my time as we moved in a circular pattern. He stumbled in his assault, just once, but it was enough for me. I shifted my weight down, swinging my blade overhead and through his exposed neck.

Panting, I watched his pathetic body turn to ash. "And that makes me Queen Bitch, motherfucker."

"Olivia, Olivia, did you hear me?" Logan asked, shaking my shoulder slightly.

"Sorry, no, what's up?" I shook my head, clearing away memories of my past.

Logan gave me a searching look and I felt the question on his lips before he changed his mind. "Vargas has requested a private meeting with us."

I looked around, not seeing said person doing the inviting. "Who told you?"

He leveled me with an annoyed look.

"Right, shifter hearing. Let's go."

I stood and Logan followed my lead, taking my hand and weaving us in between the elegantly dressed guests until we arrived in front of the woman in the gold dress.

She looked up from her clipboard, clearly shocked.

"Why, hello, I ... I was just going to speak with you," she tried to recover with a laugh.

"We know," I told her with a shrug. I wasn't going to put effort into coming up with a lie.

"Yes ... well ... then follow me." She turned, strutting in her impossibly high heels.

I probed the mate bond, wondering if Logan was checking out her assets.

No, came the answer in my head.

I huffed a laugh, looking over at him.

"You are the only one for me," he whispered before dropping a kiss against my cheek. I warmed at the action and the words, feeling for the first time in forever that things might actually be okay.

We were shown into a room designed in soft peach and gold tones. Everything about it bespoke of too much fucking money.

"That was fast," Vargas said, extending his hand to each of us in turn. I shook his hand with a smile that didn't show teeth. No need to scare the new guy, yet.

I plopped myself down on the canary flowered couch with a grunt. Logan followed, far more refined.

"Logan, thank you for coming and for your generous donation," Vargas began. "I don't believe we have had the pleasure," he said to me.

"I'm Olivia, head of the Supernatural Council for the Eastern U.S.," I clipped out.

He nodded. "You look different from the TV."

I shrugged.

"So, I imagine we need to discuss how to handle this situation," Vargas began, unbuttoning his jacket.

"What situation?" Logan asked, unbuttoning his suit jacket in turn, resting an arm over my shoulders.

"Continuing the monitoring of your kind." As though it was a given.

I scoffed, "Oh man, that's not going to happen."

"I don't see how it can't. Now, we won't move forward with the implanted tracking devices until next year."

I laughed, hard, holding my stomach and leaning forward.

"Oh man, that was funny, good one."

"I'm exceptionally serious. As we have seen, your kind can't be trusted."

"No, vampires can't be trusted. We risked life and limb to save your pathetic human asses," I reminded him.

"We didn't need your help. You brought this mess to our door."

"Nope, I sure didn't."

Vargas sat back. He had no proof for his claim and this conversation was clearly not going as he expected.

"It's going to be a law, you won't disobey the law."

I groaned, leaning my head back against Logan's arm. "You want to try and talk some sense into him?"

Logan freed his arm and I adjusted in my seat as he leaned forward, hands clasped together. "What Olivia is trying to say is that we have been protecting the humans from Supernatural threats, like the rogues. Alienating our kind will only expose this city to vampire control, without anyone or anything to protect you."

"Threats? That's how you people function?" Vargas demanded, a flush creeping up his neck.

"It's not a threat," I chimed back in. "It's the truth. You have to trust us to protect the city from threats that aren't human." Wonderful, and with that I'm back to sounding like a comic book. "Which we have proven we'll do."

"You are dangerous. I don't even know what you are," he said to me.

I shrugged, "That's not any of your business."

Vargas stood forcefully out of his chair, beginning to pace the room, "You people are monsters! Innocent people lost their lives because of you things!"

"Again, that was the vampires. We were trying to help people," I reminded him yet again. "We aren't the bad guys in this situation; however, they are coming."

"What?" he demanded.

I shook my head. "For whatever reason, the vampires have decided to target St. Ann. The Vampire High Council is en route as we speak."

"I'll deny them entry."

Logan laughed. "They can glamour almost all humans, they have super strength and blinding speed. How do you plan on doing that?"

Vargas ground his jaw.

"Look, we need you as much as you need us. We need you to continue to push for Supernaturals to have all the same rights as humans. We need you to help people understand we are not all bad, and not all of us are good, either. You need us to keep Supernatural threats who would feed on this city at bay." I crossed my arms, looking at him.

He waved a dismissive hand. "There are other issues."

"What other issues?" Logan asked.

"The adoption records for the children in your care. Many of them lack proper documentation, leaving me to wonder if you really are their guardians. Child Protection Services believes that I should relocate the children into a foster home until their real parents can be found and proper guardianship established."

"You touch my children and I will make you eat your balls," I hissed at him. He reached down to cup the anatomy in question.

"What Olivia means is, the children are going nowhere, and if you try to use them as a bargaining chip again, we will let the Vampire High Council play whatever sick and twisted games they have in mind for your town."

"It's your town, too."

"We can relocate," I hissed.

"So that's it? I do what you two demand or suffer your wrath? Why are you collecting all those children?" His eyes narrowed at us.

"Not our wrath, our lack of protection," Logan clarified. "And raising them, well."

"This isn't the Mafia," Vargas countered. "Rules need to be followed."

"No, we are far more organized, but the idea is the same," I answered him with a shrug.

"I won't agree to any of this," he hissed.

"No one said you had to." I stood, about done with the conversation. "But it's in your best interest to."

I moved to the doors, feeling Logan behind me. "This isn't over!" Vargas yelled, the last of his control breaking.

"It is for now," I told him, meeting his gaze for a long moment. "Just ask Hash."

"How dare you threaten me!"

"It's not a threat, it's a reminder that not all Supernaturals behave as we do," Logan reminded him again. The man was dense.

We didn't speak as we exited the building. There was nothing to say. I could feel Logan's worry for the situation. St. Ann was the testing ground for shifters. What happened here tended to be reflected on a national scale.

"We will figure it out," I told him, waiting outside for the car to pull around.

Logan shrugged. "He has the same mentality as Hash about us, but lacks the corruption."

"They all think that way," I told him softly.

"Not everyone. Those we saved during the rogue attacks don't."

I shook my head, wishing that was enough. We had always lived beside the humans. I wished the vampires had just stayed in the fucking closet. Hell, I wished we could put all the Supernaturals back in the closet.

The ground shook under our feet. Logan and I looked at each other.

"You feel that?" I asked, my fingers itching to palm a knife.

"I do," Logan answered, looking up and into the night. I waited, hoping his keen hearing or smell would pick something up.

Turned out there was no need for shifter senses. The boom was deafening. The sound wave, or whatever the hell it was, threw us back against the building.

I groaned, dust raining down on us as I slid down onto my ass.

"What the fuck was that?" I grunted, pulling my feet under me. My phone began ringing. I was amazed it had survived in my bra.

"Becky," I answered, taking Logan's offered hand, holding the phone with my shoulder for a moment.

"Boss, you okay?" she asked worriedly.

"Yeah, just got a little knocked around. Do you know what that was?"

"No idea. The readings are off the charts, every science center monitoring … well, everything has alarms going off. The mansion and the farm, banks, everything is going off."

"The mansion?" I asked, turning my worried gaze to Logan.

He pulled out his own phone, hopefully dialing Tommy.

"Yes, I'm monitoring the camera feed and I don't see anything amiss. Hudson is getting all the kids into the panic room."

"Good." I whooshed out a breath.

Our car pulled up with a screeching of tires. "Do you need backup?" I asked Becky.

"Blue is here." She almost sounded guilty at that confession.

"Good, anything changes or you get a location, call me back."

"Will do, boss."

Logan and I climbed into the car. "Get us back to the mansion, now!" I commanded. The driver hit the gas without asking another question.

I turned to Logan, anxiously waiting for his side of the conversation.

"I know, just get them in there. Yes, I'll have Olivia call Tommy."

He must be talking to Hudson, I realized. I still had my phone out and quickly dialed Tommy.

"Olie," he whispered.

"Everyone okay?" I asked, my heart in my throat.

"Yeah, Hudson is making us go into the panic room, is that really necessary? I don't have my monitors in there."

Well, apparently everything was okay if he was worried about his monitors.

"Yes, get in there, at least until we get back. I have no idea what that was."

"Fine," he grumbled. "Everyone in, Olie's orders."

"Stay safe, we will be there soon."

"Yeah, you too," he grumbled.

The car shook and teetered dangerously on two wheels. "What the fuck?" I grumbled, leaning forward with Logan to look through the windshield.

"What the fuck is that?" I asked Logan.

The dark night sky had been pierced by a brilliant white light, clouds circling around the beam. As fast as it had appeared, it died out.

"I don't know, but get us to the mansion," Logan commanded.

The rest of the drive we spent watching the sky, searching for any sign of trouble. Part of me wanted to head to where that light had hit the ground, assuming it had hit the ground.

Logan picked up on my thoughts. "The kids should be safe in the panic room. What more could we do there?" he asked me.

I groaned. My curiosity was getting the better of me and he was making solid points.

"Let's go."

The driver looked back at us, hearing our conversation before altering our course. I was thankful Logan vetted his staff well, but I still would have preferred to have Jerry driving us.

It didn't take long before we were unable to drive any further. Apparently, we weren't the only ones who thought investigating a glowing beam in the sky was a good idea.

Exiting the vehicle, I looked around at the humans yelling, laughing and talking. Many had their phones out, recording.

"This is dangerous," I muttered.

"They are adults," Logan said, just as a child ran across our path. "We can't protect them from their own stupidity," he reminded me. Right, just from Supernaturals.

I took a long inhale, looking around for any of those, but didn't see one. At least our kind were smarter, most of the time.

Pushing through bodies, Logan and I made our way to the center where all the action was happening. In the middle of the street was one massive, lone tree.

I grabbed Logan, pulling him back, my fingers digging into his forearm. "What's wrong?" he asked.

"It's from the fucking Fae," I hissed. "We have to destroy it."

The roots of the tree were spreading, concrete and asphalt breaking under its assault.

"Fire, we need fire," I said, turning around and looking for something flammable, wishing one of us had a smoking problem.

The tree roared.

"Fuck." I pulled my blades out, looking at Logan. The crowd around us was still too stupid to know what was going on. Thick roots pulled up before slapping down again, cutting the crowds down, finally knocking sense into the idiots milling around.

Logan and I were jostled, but we kept our positions, stepping forward into the enraged tree's warpath.

"I'll keep it busy, go find us something to burn it with," I yelled at him over the din.

He growled once, expressing his dislike for my plan, or at being bossed around, but I didn't give it a second thought before running at the tree, palming blades and wishing for a sword.

I was never leaving home without one again.

Circling around the monstrosity, which stretched higher than the ten-story buildings downtown where it had landed, I searched for a face, finding a horribly disfigured one. Twin sagging eyes, seeping green fluid. I stepped back, horror and disgust shouting warnings within me. The green goop fell onto the asphalt with a sizzling sound, etching the black asphalt away.

Great, not only was it a giant walking tree, it cried acid. Fantastic. Here's hoping fire did the trick.

I ducked under a branch that swung my way.

It seemed pointless, but I kissed a blade before heaving it at one its eyes. The bark on the trunk was etched with thick lines that made me think it was damn near impenetrable. The only vulnerable things I saw were those eyes. The succubus-kissed blade hit the white of one, and an ear-piercing wail followed. The limbs flailed with the pain, knocking down buildings and normal trees in the process. Green goo dripped from the wound, hitting the asphalt and eating it away.

"Olivia, the Executioner. I have come for you," it boomed, swaying, its good eye fixed on me. The sagging mouth hung open. Thankfully, no green acid spat out of it.

"Join the club, fucker," I yelled, palming another blade. The first one was slowly being expelled in a thick river of green acid.

Wonderful, while I may have landed a blow, it certainly wasn't a killing one. Hell, it wasn't even slowing the damn thing down. Another step with massive trunks supporting and moving it. I wobbled, thrown off by its ground-pounding force. I flung another blade at the trunk, ducking down in case of more acid, which I was sorely doubting.

The blade bounced harmlessly off its thick exterior. Perfect.

Another branch came at me, and I wasn't fast enough this time, taking the blow across the midsection and hurtling across the street. Fucker moved fast for its behemoth size.

"Asshole," I painfully grunted, certain I had a cracked rib or two from that blow.

Pushing myself into a sitting position, I looked down at the road rash covering my right side. Awesome. So much for trying to disprove Logan's Olivia-ruins-all-my-fancy-clothing claim. With a grunt, I pushed to my feet, wobbly, before running at the tree stomping its way to me.

Anytime now, I thought to Logan.

Had a disagreement with a business owner, I'm on my way.

I pulled blades. Ducking under the massive branch aimed for my head, I slammed the blades down into the thick trunk. As I had hoped, the extra force behind my blades found me purchase.

I used the blades as hand holds, pulling them out and slamming them back into the trunk, which apparently didn't bother big leafy as he made his slow trek. What the hell? Wasn't he after me?

Reaching a branch, I swung myself up, pulling only one blade with me. I was right under the canopy of leaves. Blowing out a breath, I cut at the thinner branches there.

The monster screamed again, flailing and dislodging me from my branch. I fell onto the hard asphalt on my side, renewing my already vicious road rash.

Without time to groan, I rolled under the root that tried to crush me.

"Olivia, clear out!" Logan bellowed.

He didn't have to tell me twice. I hobbled to him as he threw Molotov cocktails at the beast. Terrible waste of whatever alcohol was in them, if you ask me.

The monster screamed, a high-pitched wail that rang in my ears and cut to my core. The fire quickly traveled up the rugged exterior and into the leaves.

The flames traveled rapidly, enveloping the writing tree in a swift show until all that remained was a blackened husk.

I kicked it over, coughing back the ash that tried to enter my mouth.

"Remind me to get a flamethrower from Myrtle," I told Logan.

He nodded once, picking my weight up easily as we made our way back to the car.

"It spoke to you," Logan said.

"It did," I confirmed.

"What did it want?"

I shrugged.

"Olie," Logan warned.

"It cried acid," I offered to sidetrack him.

He grunted, "That explains your back."

"But not who summoned it or had enough magic to reach the Fae," I said, my eyes drooping heavily.

"I guess you could have asked."

I grunted as Logan slipped me into the backseat of the car. The trip back was far quicker, now that the humans had cleared out.

I leaned my forearm against the front seat headrest, not wanting to put pressure on my back while Logan wrapped it up.

He ripped my dress down the back. "How bad is it?" I asked.

He grunted a noncommittal answer. "That bad," I answered myself.

I leaned my heavy head against the headrest with a groan.

...

The gates had been locked down at the mansion and the newly established guardhouse was empty. We got out of the car, carefully unlocking the side gate. The wrought iron had electricity running though it and while it wouldn't kill Logan, it would knock him out and in my wounded state, I didn't relish the idea of dragging him into the house.

Thankfully, we made it past that booby trap unharmed. Hudson stood at the front door watching us. I had a flash back to Grams doing the same. I trampled the emotions down quickly.

"You made the news again," he said.

I grunted, pushing past him.

"Infirmary," Logan commanded, guiding me into the small medical room we had set up on the first floor, since someone was always getting hurt and ruining her clothing.

I looked back at Logan; aside from a minor blood stain, his outfit was relatively unharmed. Not fair.

"Next time, I get the fire and you distract."

Logan laughed as I sat down on the metal table. He stripped out of his jacket, rolling up his sleeves before pulling down gauze, cleaner and tape from the shelves.

I sprawled on my stomach, resting my chin on my interlaced hands.

The instant the disinfectant hit my back I tensed up, holding back a scream.

"What was that thing?" Hudson asked, poking his head in. It was quickly followed by, "Can I let the kids out?"

"I don't know," Logan answered. "And yes. We didn't see any more."

Hudson's feet retreated and I was lost in controlling my pain and my screaming until Logan finished.

"There doesn't appear to be any lingering effect in the acid," Logan said, securing the tape to my back.

I nodded, sitting up and heaving a sigh while he went to put everything away.

"Never a dull moment," I told Logan with a smile as he finished and turned to help me down.

I plopped down to my feet, regretting my lack of grace. I was moving slowly around the corner when Tommy spotted me.

"Olivia!" he yelled, barreling into me.

"Let go!" I yelled, pushing him back hurriedly, resting my hands on my knees, panting from the pain.

"She got attacked by a monster who dripped acid," Logan explained, "and tossed her around like a rag doll."

"Are you okay?" Tommy asked worriedly, bending down to look at me.

"Yeah, sorry buddy. Just tired. I need to rest and heal," I told him, straightening.

He nodded as I looked up and saw my father and Doyle coming down the stairs.

"You two, in my office." I commanded.

They looked at each other before turning around and retreating back up the stairs.

"It's our office," Logan corrected.

"That just doesn't sound as cool," I told him, fighting my way up the stairs.

With a groan and a heavy exhale, I dropped into a chair. "A tree from the fucked up world of the Fae showed up tonight in the middle of the city."

My father nodded. "We saw it on the TV."

"How the fuck is that possible?" I asked.

"I don't know. To move such a large and cherished object would take great magic and energy."

"Why send a cherished object here?" Logan asked.

The Magician shrugged. "I don't know. It takes eons for the trees to grow, they are keepers of powerful magic in their realm."

"It knew Olivia's name," Logan added.

The Magician's eyed widened, his sea green gaze resting on me. "What did it want?"

"I don't know, I was too busy trying to stay alive. The damn thing almost took out an entire block," I complained.

"Hmm," my father mused.

"She needs her powers," Doyle rumbled. It wasn't the first time he had made that claim.

The Magician sighed, "And I am not healed enough to obtain my books."

"I have an idea on that," I proposed. "What do you know about the djinn?"

My father shared a wary look with Doyle. "Not much, except that they are powerful and dangerous."

I huffed, pulling out my phone. "Yeah. I have one."

"You have a djinn?" my father asked, shocked.

"I killed his master and he became mine. Apparently, freeing a djinn ends in death. So I've been stuck with him."

I had made Amin get a phone and check in periodically. You know, just to be sure he hadn't gone off the deep end and enslaved an entire town. So far, he had continued to check in and all was well in his black-market art dealings.

He answered on the third ring.

"Olivia, no I did not send a giant tree to your town."

"Well that's reassuring, but not why I am calling."

"Do tell." Amin sounded interested, in a bored, I've-lived-forever way.

"Can you help a magician boost his powers to open a portal to where the succubi are held prisoner?" I asked.

Amin paused. "That was a loaded sentence. To answer the question, yes I can."

"What about the return trip?" I asked. "How long will you need to rest to open it again and bring me back?"

Amin cleared his throat. "A day, maybe two at the most."

I nodded. "When can you get to St. Ann?"

"I'll need a few days to get my affairs in order."

"Do it, and get here. There's no telling what else is going to shoot from the sky."

"I will do so," he answered before hanging up.

"You can trust him?" my father asked, voicing Logan's concerns pinging around in my head.

"You have another option?" I asked, flicking my gaze to Logan to include him in my response.

"We could wait," Doyle offered.

"Right, then how long would I be trapped in the red world until you would be strong enough to bring me back?"

Doyle had no answer for that and looked to The Magician for help.

"At least a week, and I wouldn't be able to keep the portal open long if you missed the opportunity," he finally admitted.

I rubbed my forehead. I still had the fucking vampires to deal with, not to mention whoever the hell had called up that damn portal to drop the oversized tree.

"Can you figure out a way to track the portal from tonight?" I asked my father.

He shook his head and I groaned. "I guess I should have asked a few more questions of the talking tree."

Logan gave an annoyed huff, agreeing. I narrowed my eyes at him.

"I need to eat and rest," I said with a sigh, standing and turning to walk out.

"Olivia," my father called out, "what about your mother?"

"What about her?" I asked, facing him.

He rose. "You are going to leave her behind?" he pushed, his posture held stiff.

"What would you prefer me to do? Kill her?" I'd have really liked to do that.

"She may regain her senses if allowed to escape."

I groaned, rubbing the back of my neck. "Look, I don't know what happened exactly to get everyone thrown into that hellhole of a dimension, but what I do know is that she and you sold me into slavery. So I don't feel any lingering maternal attachment to the bitch."

He didn't like that answer, but I wasn't backing down. If I hadn't needed him to escape from the red hell, I'm not sure I would have saved him, either. Even if he was growing on me, a little.

His jaw ground out the usually unspoken words between us, "Will you ever forgive me for that?"

I sighed, my shoulders slumping. "I don't know. Some scars don't ever heal, and all the ones inflicted by Selena never have."

"I did it to save you. Look around at all you have because of what I did."

I barked out a laugh, taking a step closer to him. "You are not responsible for any of this! I crawled my way out of Selena's clutches, I built an empire, and you are riding my coattails. Do. Not. Forget. It."

With that I left. Logan's emotions were calm compared to my own tornado of shit. He lingered and while I could have tapped in to see what he was saying, I decided not to. He knew how I felt about this situation and I felt his agreement in the mate bond.

Tossing off my clothing onto the floor, I climbed into bed. Logan would take issue with me not showering, but I didn't give a shit.

Chapter 3

I woke up to arguing. The voices were too far away for me to hear what was being yelled about. Another little voice yelled out. I turned to see Ginny sitting up in her crib, deadpan staring at the monitor. With a groan, I tossed on Logan's shirt and went to pick up the princess.

My back pulled, but it felt better—not perfect, but hopefully before Amin showed up I'd be back to normal. Whatever normal was for me.

Padding down the stairs with a changed and clean baby, I heard Jerry yelling, "Why didn't you call me?"

"It wasn't my decision," Logan hollered back.

"The djinn are not to be trusted!" Jerry yelled.

"Enough," I said softly, rounding into the kitchen. "I did what I had to, Jerry. We don't know what was powerful enough to open a portal and bring over a massive killing tree. I'm not going to sit by when I need to access the rest of my power."

"Why didn't you call me?" Jerry pleaded as I set Ginny in her highchair.

"It's not your decision to make," I echoed Logan's earlier words. "Do you have access to a coven I don't know about?"

Jerry's mouth shut quickly before he shook his head.

"I'm aware it's a gamble. Worst case, I get stuck in the red hell for a week and I kill Amin on my return trip," I told Jerry with a shrug.

He shook his head, still not liking it.

"I kill Amin," Logan corrected.

I laughed, "Fine, I'll give you that one."

"How's your back?" Logan asked.

"Better, hopefully when Amin shows up I'll be back to fighting shape."

Logan nodded and we passed the rest of breakfast in silence. Having nothing on the schedule, we settled on the couch while Ginny played with her toys.

...

I had fallen asleep in the nursery rocking chair with a warm, sleeping Ginny nestled on my chest. Logan's potent concern cascaded through the mate bond and jerked me awake. Blinking to clear my exhausted gaze, I carefully eased Ginny down into her crib and headed to our office after grabbing her monitor.

I found Logan staring intently at his computer.

"What's wrong?" I asked, rubbing sleep from my eyes, setting down the baby monitor on his desk.

"Mal is at the gate," he rumbled, his caramel gaze pinning me.

I went to stand behind him, leaning over his shoulder and seeing her standing next to a dark vehicle. She had her left arm across her stomach, then shifted her weight and shoved both of her hands into her jacket pockets. Her shoulders arched forward before she finally settled, her arms crossed over her chest.

"She's nervous. Who else is in the car?" I asked.

"She said friends," Logan answered.

"What did you tell her?"

"That with the unrest with the vampires, we will meet them outside the gate."

I nodded. "Let's not keep our guest waiting."

Logan hadn't bothered to change out of his track pants. I had pulled on jeans, a bra, a black top, dual guns, a sword, and throwing knives—just your usual casual attire for quiet day at home. I still needed to call Myrtle about a damn flamethrower.

Logan raised a caramel eyebrow at me as I stomped down the steps next to him to the front door. "Really?" He asked.

"Really. Did you give Ali the baby monitor?" I had checked the office, but hadn't seen it.

He nodded.

"Alright, let's go greet our friends." I rubbed my hands together, equal parts excited and nervous. We had extended Mal protection, but that didn't mean she couldn't be used as bait to lure us out and kill us.

Mal and I had met at Kitten. She worked security there part time, when not working her full-time security gig at the Centennial House, which no longer existed.

Logan and I had granted her protection when she gave her blood to save Ginny. It was a complicated relationship, to say the least. Especially since Logan had killed Tate, who Mal had confessed to be in love with. Tate had known

Zachariah's plans to kidnap me and done nothing. His death was to be expected.

Logan and I stopped in front of the guard gate, using the small door to the side. He held the door while I walked through, arms crossed, smile lacking.

"Finally," Mal complained, forcing a smile. "I tried explaining to this guy who I was." She waved at the guard gate.

"He knows who you are," I told her, relaxing my arms. "Who's in the car?" I tilted my chin at the black and expensive town car.

"Friends, they want to meet you," Mal said, her shifting gaze and wavering voice only confirming what I had seen on the monitor.

"Well, here I am." I opened my arms, letting them fall with an irritated thud.

"It's a little exposed," Mal tried, casting a look around. I could just feel her reaching for an excuse to get the unknown vampire into my house. Not going to happen.

I sighed. "Look Mal, I get it. You have to do what they say, but I'm done playing games and since the assholes in the car can hear that, they have sixty seconds to show themselves or get off my lawn." Alright, technically my driveway, well our driveway, but whatever.

The driver's door opened, and Mal moved quickly to get out of the way.

A towering, thin vampire with aviator glasses and a skinny black tie and black suit stepped out, unfolding his body slowly from the town car. I was seriously wondering how he had fit.

He closed the door silently, his face drawn. I was registering zero emotion from him. I took a step closer to Logan; this guy was creeping me the hell out.

"This is Igor," Mal said submissively, "Summoner of the Vampire High Council."

I felt Logan's irritation and annoyance, or maybe that was my own?

"Executioner, Alpha." Igor slightly bowed. "I am here to collect you for the Vampire High Council," he said, removing his glasses to reveal washed out blue eyes.

"Sure, just let us get our car." I started to back away.

"No. I will take you," Igor stated in the same inflectionless tone.

"That's not going to work," I said, resting my hands on my hips.

"This is the way it is done."

39

"Not on my turf, especially not after the shit we've gone through with vamps. I'll agree to meeting on your terms, but no way in hell am I giving up my ability to leave."

Igor had no words. Apparently, people didn't say no to him often.

"I will need to make a call," he finally came up with.

"Feel free." Logan and I shared a look, neither of us expecting this to end well.

Mal came to stand with us. "Are you alright?" Logan asked.

She nodded, casting a fearful glance over her shoulder. "Raphael assured me they wouldn't harm me, and that going against their wishes would be far worse."

I nodded, "Good. We haven't heard from him."

"He was ordered to stay out of it," Mal shrugged.

"Not unexpected," Logan commented, watching the dark vehicle closely.

I doubted Igor was actually stupid enough to call; he was probably texting.

Are we doing this? Logan asked.

I don't know. We don't owe them anything. It's certainly a risk, but leaving them to stew is almost worse.

Logan nodded and Igor opened his door.

"They will allow you to follow us," he announced. I rolled my eyes.

"Wonderful," I groaned. I turned, heading back through the iron gate and to the garage.

"You need anything else?" Logan asked.

I shrugged. "I never called Myrtle for my flamethrower."

Logan laughed, using the fingerprint scanner followed by the keypad to open the large garage door.

"I didn't think you were serious about that," he said, heading to my SUV.

"I was exceptionally serious. I actually wonder why I haven't gotten one sooner."

I felt Logan's gaze on me as I slipped into the passenger seat. "What?"

"A flamethrower? Where are we going to keep that?" Logan asked logically.

"The garage?"

"Our insurance policy can't handle that," he complained, setting the car into drive after watching the garage door close firmly.

I patted his shoulder. "Don't worry, honey, I can afford it."

He laughed, waiting for the iron gates to open.

"I guess I should let everyone know what's going on," I muttered, calling Ali.

She answered immediately. "Are you going?" she demanded.

I tilted my head, confused. "How did you know?"

"Um, Tommy and I were listening."

I should have guessed. "Yes, we are going. Flood the gates with electricity once we leave. I don't trust these fuckers."

"Then why are you going?" Tommy bit out. He was not doing well with this—Grams's death, me leaving.

"I'm hoping that dealing with them head on will eliminate problems down the road," I told him honestly.

"The vampires can't be trusted," he reminded me in an annoyed tone.

"I'm aware, but we are all Supernaturals in the end. I'm taking the meeting." End of discussion, kid.

"Fine," Tommy grunted. "I'll be tracking you."

"I'd expect nothing less. And get Mal a ride back to Raphael, please," I added. Normally, I'd have her go inside with the kids, but not right now. I hoped I could trust her again some day, but I knew the damage had been done. What if we hadn't refused her entrance past the gate? Would she have brought Igor into my home with the children? I didn't want to think about that.

I terminated the call, sitting back with a sigh. "It's possible he is still listening. He has pulled that trick on me more than once," Logan warned warily.

I laughed. "Ugh, sometimes I wonder if I fucked up bringing him into the Council's business."

Logan adjusted his seat, and I knew he wondered the same thing. "You think he is too young," I stated. It wasn't a question.

Logan sighed. "How did you meet Tommy?"

"I didn't meet him, I rescued him," I answered, looking out the window. "It was shortly after I had taken over the Council. I had Grams handcuffed in the bathroom to get her to sober up." The memory caused a painful cut across my heart; I pushed on, clearing my throat. "An anonymous tip came in that this woman posing as a foster parent was taking 'gifted' children and selling them off."

41

"Gifted?" Logan questioned.

"Succubi, sirens, and a few diluted demigods."

"Powerless groups."

I grunted my annoyance and agreement. "Anyways, I needed a break from babysitting Grams, so I went to investigate."

I could still remember the stench from that rundown farm. There wasn't a great way to approach it in secret. I opted for waiting until close to midnight—darkness would give me cover, and if I was caught, midnight wasn't an unusual time to be out for a Supernatural. The farm was located almost two hours from the mansion, far outside the city. The simple, ranch-style home was well kept up, the front porch lit up by the powerful light above the front door.

I stepped out of my black car and an old hound dog raised his head, looking over at me with disinterest before lying back down.

My steps were loud against the crisp grass. The front steps groaned under my approach. I knocked on the powder blue screen door, the boom echoing loudly before I stepped back, flexing my hands. I really needed a good fight.

Voices yelled inside. Amidst the scuffling, a small head peeked up, pushing the flowered curtain out of the way to look me over from the window.

I should have scared the dark haired and dark skinned boy that looked over my dual swords, leather jacket, and throwing knives strapped to my thigh. His ebony eyes looked into my own, not with excitement as I thought a young kid should, but with knowledge far beyond his years.

His head disappeared and there was a loud thump. My gaze jerked up to the dark haired, pale skinned woman who replaced him.

"You ain't got no business here," she said through the window, not opening the door.

"That assumes you know who I am," I answered softly.

"You with the city."

"Nope."

"I'm outside the city limits. These kids mine."

I tilted my head. "Open the door."

"Naw, you get out of here or I'll call the cops."

I shrugged, "Go ahead."

The human police didn't scare me, even if they were annoying.

She took another look over my clothing. "You ain't with the foster department."

I smiled, "Nope."

She swallowed and I could scent her sweat and fear. "Who—who you with?"

"My name is Olivia. I am head of the Supernatural Council. I've had a complaint that you have what is mine."

Her eyes widened. "The Council, I thought — I thought — a vampire runs them."

"A vampire ran it," I corrected, leaning against the glass separating us.

"I'm human," she recovered, brushing back her oily hair. "You can't touch me."

I gave her a soft laugh, straightening up before I punched through the glass and clamped down around her throat.

"Gotcha," I whispered to her purpling form...

I cleared my throat and turned to Logan, pushing the rest of those memories away.

"It turned out a human had in fact figured out a way to tell who was Supernatural, and was selling them for pay for play."

"How old was Tommy?" Logan asked, disgust and horror filtering through the mate bond.

"Eight," I answered. "He had never gone to school, never had anyone be kind to him. He wouldn't even speak for the first year."

"How did you get him to come around?" Logan asked, seamlessly following the vampires in front of us.

"Video games. I was picking up pizza and he became entranced with this arcade game. I must have spent a hundred dollars that night, eating the pizza as he played. As soon as I had enough money, I bought him every game system he ever wanted."

Logan nodded. "I didn't realize."

I shrugged, watching the tail lights of the vampires at a red light.

"I found Connie there, too, chained down to a bed in the basement," I added.

Logan sighed, "Do they all have such stories?"

"Yes," I answered. "Every last one of them has some horrific past. I suppose that's why I'm drawn to them."

Logan reached over, pulling my hand into his as he made the left turn with one hand.

"Your father seems intent on saving your mother."

I grunted in agreement. "I'm not saving her."

"I know," Logan answered.

"She sold me into slavery."

"I know."

"She's a monster and I plan on killing her." I hadn't actually known I had made that decision.

"Are you going to tell your father?"

"No. He doesn't need to know." It was easier to ask forgiveness than permission. Assuming I wanted his forgiveness.

Logan nodded. He didn't agree with me, but it was my decision and he respected it.

"Where do you think they are taking us?" I asked, changing the subject.

Logan shrugged. "Somewhere with impressive security."

"It's gotta be somewhere where they can maintain their anonymity," I mused.

Logan made the final turn, slowing down in front of a skyrise. Igor turned into the parking garage.

"Or they like their amenities more than practicality," Logan observed.

"Fucking vampires." I should have known.

Igor was waiting for us at the elevator of the parking structure, still no emotion on his weathered face. Logan and I stepped into the elevator without a word when it arrived. We made it to ground level, where we were waved past the front desk security with a wary stare, and finally into another set of elaborately decorated elevators.

"You will have to leave your weapons before we enter," Igor said when the doors of the elevator opened at the tenth floor.

I stayed in the elevator when he exited. "You can pry them out of my cold, dead hands."

Igor's jaw clenched. "Why is everything so difficult with you?"

"Perks of my personality," I answered, letting the door close. Igor stopped them with a loud thump.

"Fine, bring your weapons, but know it is an insult," he growled.

"Can't say I give a shit," I answered, strutting out. We turned left toward closed doors, where another vampire stood guard.

He moved aside without a word. The double doors opened, and scantily clad humans stood on either side, their pupils dilated. I groaned as we entered the lair.

Lair was the appropriate word: silk and organza disguised the ceiling in sweeping scallops. Long pieces hung down, giving the illusion of privacy as hushed whispers and cries of delight seeped out from the shelters.

Logan and I shared a disbelieving and annoyed look. Setting up a fucking lair in my town—nope, not going to happen.

"Follow me," Igor said, making his way expertly to the back left. Logan and I followed, my hands itching to pull back a few of those pieces of silk to see exactly what the fuck was going on. I didn't appreciate my vision being hampered.

Igor held up a piece of thick black silk before unlocking a door and ushering us into a library.

I turned to find an empty room and Igor shutting the door.

"If they fucking make me wait," I hissed.

"Executioner," said a voice coming from behind the stacks. "I am Eduardo."

"What the fuck do you think you are doing in my territory?" I hissed as my eyes settled on him.

Logan's hand on my shoulder stopped me from shoving Eduardo in his stupid black silk robe.

"Have I broken a law?" he asked innocently.

I growled.

"These are humans, here of their own free will and suffering no harm."

"Oh fucker, you can play this game, but know when you step out of line I will end you."

"Enough," he clipped out forcefully. "I will not be threatened in my own home by such a pathetic excuse for a leader. I will have your Council as a plaything if I so wish."

Logan released me and stepped up next to me. "Watch your mouth, vampire. The humans in this town are not fans of your poor management of the Houses, nor are we. I've already killed two master vampires this year, and I'd have no problem with adding a third."

Eduardo hissed, "You're both disrespectful."

I had nothing to say to that, apparently neither did Logan.

"I brought you both here to discuss the repairs you must make in order to fix the mess you've made." He sat behind his regal desk, elbows perched on the armrests, fingertips touching in front of him.

I laughed, sitting down in a black high-backed chair. Logan sat on the arm and the chair groaned. Clearly, we were going to be there a while setting the record straight.

I stayed silent, wanting to hear exactly what the asshole thought we needed to do. "Due to your hasty execution of Tate and Zachariah, we are left with numerous vampires without a Master, and Raphael's Houses"—heavy emphasis on the plural—"have doubled in size."

"So?" I asked, none of that concerning me.

"The masterless will need to be collected." He flexed his long, wrinkled fingers, scowling at me, his thick brown eyebrows drawn over his equally brown eyes.

"Not a problem, send over our retainer and I'll put an executioner on it," I told him with a shrug.

Eduardo blinked at me, confused. These fuckers did not hear "no" often.

"We are happy to assist you, but as Olivia has said, our help comes at a price," Logan clarified.

"You would dare charge ME to fix your mistakes?" He was genuinely offended, his hands growing nails that dug into the soft Italian leather of his chair as he leaned forward.

I laughed. "We didn't make any mistakes. You did and you keep making them. We aren't here to bow down and give you false worship, we are here to see how the fuck you plan on fixing your mess."

"We have a meeting with the potential new Governor." He regained his composure, nails retracting.

"Good luck," Logan grunted.

I nodded. "We didn't have much success in that realm."

"Yes, well, I am not surprised. You lack tact and any political sense." I don't think he could have tilted his nose any higher in the air.

I rolled my eyes. "Wonderful, so we came all this way just to be insulted?"

Eduardo said nothing to that.

I'm about done here, I sent to Logan.

Blake and Angelina are here, he sent back.

That had my eyes widening. What are they doing here?

I don't know, but I can hear them outside the doors planning on surprising you.

I groaned. Date one vampire and never hear the end of it.

"If that is all?" Logan asked.

Eduardo gave us a dismissive wave. "We will be in touch."

I was certain he would be, since he clearly couldn't handle his own fucking masterless vampire problem. I was charging him double for being a dick.

Logan opened the door. I stepped through it and around Blake and Angelina hanging in a swing of silk suspended from the ceiling, naked.

I gave thought to making a comment as their bodies intertwined and rubbed against each other. There was a whole diatribe of horrid and caustic one-liners running on repeat in my head. I even opened my mouth, having selected the one I deemed best, but I just shook my head and kept walking. Blake meant nothing to me. Logan filled the void he had left and overflowed my soul with emotions the vampire could never inspire in me.

I just didn't care anymore, though that didn't mean I was above killing them.

We passed through the doors, the same drugged-up females letting us out. I didn't see Igor and I didn't care to, either.

In the elevator, I leaned back with a sigh, resting my head against the spotless glass. I was secretly hoping I left an oily smudge.

"What?" Logan asked, pressing the opaque white DOWN button before coming to lean back against the glass with me. I looked up at him, wondering if he'd heard my earlier, unspoken thought.

I shook my head, dismissing the childish worry and answering his question. "We're getting pushback a lot. I'm not used to it. I've become too soft if both the vamps and the humans think they can railroad me."

Logan chuckled, "No Blake and Angelina comment?"

I leaned into his shoulder. "Nope, you are the only one I want to see naked."

He hung a heavy arm around me, pulling me close. "Right answer," he whispered into my ear.

I wrapped my arms around his waist. "Can't we just kill them all?" I asked hopefully, looking up into those caramel depths.

Logan sighed, "Unfortunately not."

I groaned, "Then it's going to be interesting."

Chapter 4

True to his word, Amin showed up exactly two days after our conversation. Logan and I were in our office, looking over the limited documents we were able to obtain from Grams's lawyer.

"The widow is taking over operation of Kitten," Logan said, pushing the papers across his desk to me. I scanned them, a sinkhole forming in my chest.

"Maybe it's time to move on from dance clubs," I sighed.

"What are you going to open next, a daycare?" Logan teased, trying to lighten my mood.

"Sure, Junior Executioner Camp: While you work, I'll teach your kids how to shoot, kill, and maim."

Logan laughed. I thought the idea actually had merit.

The air pressure in the room condensed, my ears popped, and there appeared Amin, sitting regally next to me in a suit that was possibly more expensive then my gun collection.

Logan growled, not appreciating the show of power. I just shrugged; if he had the ability to do that, he could have killed us at any point. Granted, Jerry said Amin was unable to kill me directly. I had asked him once for the long laundry list of what Amin could do, and it quickly became apparent it would be easier to list the things he couldn't do.

"You are certain you wish to travel to the red world?" Amin asked, not bothering with pleasantries as he unfastened the gold button of his suit jacket. I don't think expensive was the right word for his clothing choices. Opulent, possibly; over the top, definitely.

"Yep, sure am," I answered in my yoga pants.

Amin nodded. "I'll go get The Magician," Logan said, standing and glaring at Amin the entire way around his desk.

I stood. "I'm going to prepare. I'll be damned if I'm surviving on moldy bread and cheese again."

Logan looked down at me outside the doorway as I closed the door behind me. I could read the determination in his gaze not to lose me again. I had ventured once to that world, and sending me back there wasn't sitting well.

"If it makes you feel any better, I don't want to go, either," I offered with a shrug. His brow only furrowed further.

I pulled him down and kissed him, infusing it with all the love my damaged soul could carry.

"I will always come back for you," I told him, standing on tiptoe and searching that raw sienna gaze, hoping my message reached home.

He stroked my back my strawberry blond locks. "I know. I just don't relish you traveling somewhere that I can't."

I nodded. "Someone has to keep the kids in line." We both had control issues.

He huffed out a breath.

"Besides, I've already been there once. How hard can it be to grab a few dusty books?" I asked with a shrug, trying to minimize the danger. One exceptionally pissed off mother, check. Unicorns and mermaids I wasn't prepared to bring over, check. No Magician or Doyle to guide me through ... okay, now I was just depressing myself.

Logan kissed my forehead, one large, warm palm cupping my cheek. He pulled back to look deeply into my eyes. "I have never loved another the way my heart belongs to you, Olivia. I trust that not even death could keep us apart."

"Oh, stop it." I pushed him in the direction of my father, blinking away the tears. Damn emotional shifter.

I heard his soft laughter behind me as I headed to our room to get changed.

...

Anna was waiting for me outside my room. I raised an eyebrow at Ginny perched on her hip.

"I thought you'd want to say goodbye," she said, handing me the quiet baby.

"You are correct," I said, holding Ginny close, kissing her chubby cheek. "I'm surprised she let you hold her."

Anna shrugged, not meeting my gaze. "They're growing on me."

I nodded, understanding.

"It helps," I added softly.

Her ice blue eyes were conflicted when she looked back at me. "I thought if I could just forget about it all, pretend it didn't happen, I'd be better off. But now, now I look at these kids and see the survivor I wish I could have been."

I nodded. I didn't need words, I understood perfectly.

Finally I said, "They're resilient, partly because they have to be and partly because they have us."

Anna nodded, clearing her throat. "Anyways, I wanted to see if I could come with you."

My eyes widened in surprise. "You want to?"

She nodded, "I want to see our home."

"We will have to check with The Magician, to see if he has the energy to send us both back."

She nodded. "Your father," she clarified.

I sighed, rocking Ginny when she started to fuss. "I'm not ready to call him that on a regular basis."

We began walking downstairs to the kitchen. "Let's get our food together," was all I had to add.

...

It didn't take us long to stuff two backpacks with food, and to dress in leather that I would instantly regret once we crossed into the overheated red world. Anna strapped her dual swords to her back, matching my own.

I gave Ginny a long squeeze, inhaling her baby scent before passing her over to her nanny, Katie.

"You ready for this?" Anna asked next to me, ascending the stairs.

I shrugged. My back had healed, but my guards were just alright. "I'd rather not go back, but I need to unlock what The Magician hid from me to face what is coming."

"The Fae," Anna offered on a long, exhausted exhale. It had always been the damn Fae.

"Yes," I agreed. I wish those fuckers could stay in their own damn dimension.

We pushed into the office. Logan's gaze flicked over us, noting our similar dress and weapons. Relief washed through the mate bond as he realized Anna was trying to come along. Maybe this would win her his trust.

"You both will be traveling through the portal?" Amin asked, his obsidian gaze flicking between the two of us.

"If you can handle it," Anna taunted, a wicked smile curving her blood red lips. I'd have to ask her how she kept her lipstick so damn perfect.

The Magician nodded. "It might take longer for us to bring you back, but we can send you both. Just be certain to be touching each other when the portal opens. Now, you are clear on what books I need?"

"Yes, you've recited the list several times, made me repeat it, and given it to Anna in writing." I was not acknowledging that I sounded like a petulant child. "Where are we doing this?"

"Here," Logan said, coming around his desk. "Jerry warded the room. He said keeping the energy contained will be easier here than outside."

I nodded, meeting his raw sienna gaze and tramping down the voice screaming at me not to leave him, again. I pushed out a shaky breath. This had to be done. I had no other choice.

Logan stepped in close, brushing his fingers against my cheek. He gave me a small smile, feeling my hesitation and our shared worry. Blowing out a breath, I focused on the two magic users in the room. I was glad Jerry wasn't here. I didn't need his judgment on my trust in Amin.

"Shall we?" Amin said to The Magician.

My father nodded. As pouches were dumped out onto the once clean coffee table, I heard Logan's internal groan. The various herbs were ground up and fragrant. The Magician and the djinn shared a look, a nod passing between them before they began chanting. I didn't understand the whispered words, but I felt the power flooding the room. My skin prickled, goose bumps running along my spine.

I took Anna's hand, tiptoeing to kiss Logan one last time. My lips had hardly brushed his stubbled cheek when the portal sucked Anna and me backwards.

I didn't have time to scream. What little air my lungs held was trapped, my chest unable to inflate. I was going to die in this tunnel of brilliant colors. Anna's hand became the only thing that grounded me and kept me sane, her fingers digging in just as strongly as my own.

My body was certain it was being ripped apart. My ears heard nothing but the constant whoosh around us. I wanted nothing more than a release from the constant pressure.

As quickly as it began, it stopped.

I sucked in a breath, still refusing to let go of Anna's hand. I could feel the rough pebbles under my palms and sticking into my forehead. I wheezed, sucking in the dirt I knew was red, well I really hoped it was.

"Can you see?" Anna choked out, before falling into a fit of coughing.

"No," I answered, my voice hoarse. The light had sufficiently blinded us. I still saw imprints of the swirling colors on the black of my eyelids. I pushed into a sitting position, forcing her with me and closing my eyes for long moments. I didn't enjoy being vulnerable. Neither of us did, and being blind in an unfriendly world was a horrible idea.

Slowly, my vision returned, and I squinted at the familiar red scene. "You good?" I asked Anna.

She nodded, looking over the red dirt world around us. I hadn't found it awe inspiring the first time I saw it, and I can't imagine she did, either.

"What is this world called?" she asked, releasing my hand. I flexed my own, returning feeling to my fingertips.

"I don't know. I've just been calling it the red world." I shifted to my knees, heaving a breath before we both pushed to our feet.

Anna nodded, turning in a full circle to survey the same lotus rock formation I had found myself in not long ago.

"How do we get out?" she asked, touching the jagged rocks around us.

"Climb. Carefully, the rocks are sharp."

She nodded and we began our ascent. It was impossible not to obtain a few scratches, but neither of us needed stitches. This part had been easier when I wasn't corporeal.

"Is that it?" Anna asked, jutting her chin toward the red-stained horizon.

I looked at the Aladdin-style palace in the distance. "Yeah. That's it," I answered.

There was no one waiting to greet me with open arms this time, even if those arms wanted something.

"How will The Magician know where to open the portal?" Anna asked.

"He has my hair. It's apparently tuned in to me or something."

"Oh." She didn't sound convinced.

"I don't understand how it works," I admitted, scanning the wide expanse of maroon landscape. If we were attacked here, even with our small arsenal, we would be running to the palace.

"But you need to," Anna reminded me.

I sighed. "Yeah, I'm going to be getting a crash course in how to be a magician's daughter here, I suppose." Note that I was not excited about it.

"Are you going to forgive him?" Anna asked with a mix of curiosity and heavy sarcasm. Forgiveness wasn't an act we performed often or really at all.

"I'm not sure I can," I told her honestly.

Anna nodded. "He's your father."

I grunted, "He sold me."

Anna said nothing more on the subject, but she didn't stay silent as we continued our march. "So, that Mindy is a pistol."

I huffed with a laugh, "That she is."

"You are going to have your hands full with that one."

"She's human. Mercer is going to have his hands full."

Anna laughed. Then, after a pause, "What happened to her parents?"

"I don't know. I found her chained in a basement with two sick fuckers. Mercer is her legal guardian now."

Anna nodded, and we continued on in silence.

...

Logan stared for long moments at the spot where Olivia and Anna had been standing, hearing his own heartbeat rushing in his ears, listening to his beast's painful wails. Feeling his lion clawing, writhing to be free. To kill and maim until his mate was returned to him. He pulled in another long breath, shaking his head in hopes of clearing it.

He exhaled, long and slow. Olivia would be okay. She had traveled that world once before, she would come back to him, to their life, to their children. She would come back. Logan took another breath, finding he could hear again.

He turned to survey the room, finding the Magician and Amin unconscious and sprawled across the coffee table, herbs scattered everywhere.

"Where's the damn vacuum?" he muttered.

...

Anna and I arrived at the palace without difficulty, entering as I had previously, through the broken window in the forgotten nursery.

"Whoa," Anna said softly, turning around. I gave the obviously well loved but dusty nursery a quick glance before I moved to the door. We didn't have time to waste, and I needed to see who exactly we were going to be up against.

I waited a moment until I felt Anna next to me, then drew my sword with a silent pull. I needed its weighty presence before I opened the door. I did so slowly, peering into the cardinal, murky darkness. No torches illuminated the way; the shadows were thick. Anyone or anything could have been hiding, waiting for us, having seen us in the wide open, trekking to the only structure on that miserable world.

Anna took her post next to me, watching my expression closely. "What is it?" she hissed.

I shook my head. "There is no light. Last time I was here, torches were kept," I answered softly.

Anna shrugged, "No time like the present to find out why."

I exhaled, she was correct. I pushed the door open, giving one last look to the shadows before I moved out of Anna's way, waiting until she quietly closed the door before moving down the hallway and toward The Magician's work room.

Anna followed me on silent feet. My eyes adjusting to the red gloom, I kept my steps slow and measured, careful of half-opened doors and turnoffs. Nothing ill met us, and I pushed open the broken door of The Magician's workroom cautiously.

The wooden workbench was broken in half, the cot I had slept on torn to shreds. The various cubbies above the workbench had been tossed every which way, the contents destroyed. I turned, seeing the tall bookshelf, empty.

"Well, fuck," I hissed, just barely restraining myself from stomping my foot.

"Someone was sure pissed," Anna commented, picking up The Magician's magnifying glass, the glass shattered and the frame bent.

"To say the least," I muttered, noting the shredding of the cot. Had talons done that, or just a pissed off succubus?

"What now?" Anna questioned, moving a piece of debris with her foot.

I mashed my lips together. "He said The Queen kept powerful texts in her chambers. Maybe she moved everything there." It was a long shot and we both knew it. The warding on The Magician's door should have kept everyone out.

"What's the game plan?" Anna asked.

"Walking the fuck in," I answered, running a hand over my weapons before I met her gaze. "Get ready to meet our mother. Then I'm killing her."

I turned away from Anna's expression of shock, followed closely by anger. Encountering our mother was going to leave her bitter and disappointed, just like me.

I moved the broken door loudly out of our way, refusing to sneak around anymore. There was only one way to cut the head off the snake, and it didn't involve covert games. Or maybe it did, but I wasn't playing them.

Anna jogged to catch up to me. Still no torch light; it was bothering me, nagging at me, but I wasn't giving it as much attention as I should have

We hit the throne room and I stopped, testing the weight of my still-drawn sword. The golden statues were just as they had been, but a generous coating of red dust marred their surfaces.

"Not one for cleaning?" Anna asked, touching a statue and rubbing the crimson dirt between her fingers. I watched her gaze rove over the collection, the corners of her mouth turning down.

"Something is wrong. They were in pristine condition when I was here last," I said, spinning in a slow circle. I held my breath and listened. Nothing, not a sound, not a whisper or rustle of clothing.

"Where is everyone?" Anna asked.

"I don't know." I turned away from the unkempt statues. "Come on, The Queen's chambers are down that hallway.

Anna nodded, shifting her focus, her sword in hand as we eased down the hallway. As in the throne room, scarlet dust coated the statues and the stone under our feet, puffs of dirt tickling my nose. My pace slowed and I raised my sword as we walked through heavily shadowed corners.

Red light spilled into the hallway from the large, open window. Anna stepped out of the shadows first, taking in the sex chamber of our mother, her sword dropping.

"There's no one here, Olie," she said, turning in a circle.

I grunted, coming up next to her, keeping my sword poised as I checked the bathroom and closet. Finding her announcement accurate, I went to the window, hoping for a clue, my sword still hanging from my hand.

Nothing stared back at me except the red wasteland. This just didn't make any damn sense. I finally stowed my sword.

I turned to Anna. She was looking over at the empty bookshelf along the wall parallel to the bed.

"Any other ideas on where we can find what we need?" she asked.

"No," I grumbled. "This was a fucking waste." I was ready to tear my damn hair out.

"Maybe not, the books had to go somewhere," Anna shrugged. "Do they have a library here?"

"I don't know. It's possible she took them with her when everyone left."

"Where would they have gone?" Anna asked. She sheathed her sword and we walked down the dark hallway, side by side.

"I don't know. Nowhere I went here welcomed me with open arms. Everything and everyone seemed to hate her for getting them stuck here."

Anna nodded, digesting that chunk of information silently.

"Come on, let's check this place out. Maybe we will get lucky," she said to me once we arrived back at the throne room.

"Yeah. I guess." My hopes were dashed. What did we do now? Just wait for Amin and my father to pull us back empty handed?

We cleared room after room, finding all of them in some sort of disarray, but not a single body of the dead or the living.

"This is the kitchen," I said, pushing open the door.

A pan slammed into the side of my head. "Fucker!" I yelled, dropping down, kicking out against the shin of my attacker as I rolled.

"Not another move," Anna hissed. Blinking to clear my vision, I stayed down, looking up at her sword at a tall and skinny man's throat. His clothing was stained and torn, stubble thick on his face. He swallowed, a trickle of blood seeping down from his Adam's apple.

"Back up," Anna commanded. The man dropped the pan and it landed heavily. I winced from the sound, standing up as Anna stepped into the room, the wooden door closing behind us. So much for the castle being deserted.

"Ouch," I complained, rubbing the goose egg forming near my temple.

"Who are you?" whispered a voice from the shadows.

"Olivia, and you are?" I turned, seeing a young man cowering against the wall, clutching a small bundle, his clothing just as filthy as Frying Pan Man's.

"I am Ox, this is Giv," he said, pointing, his eyes not leaving the sword poised at his buddy's throat.

"Where is everyone?" I asked, wishing I had thought to pack Tylenol in my first aid kit.

Giv's brows furrowed. "You do not know?" he asked against Anna's sword.

"We just got here," Anna said. "Enlighten us."

"The F-Fae took them all," Ox said, scooting away from the wall, carefully watching Anna.

"The Fae?" I asked, my heart beating faster. "What were the Fae doing here?"

"The Queen summoned them, made a deal with them to get everyone she wanted over to Earth," Giv supplied with heavy malice.

"The Queen is on Earth?!" My voice pitched up and my stomach dropped.

Ox nodded, "Along with the Fae."

"FUCK! We have to get back now and warn everyone." My fear spread a cold chill under my skin. Thankfully, Anna kept her calm.

"How do you plan on doing that?" she asked.

I shook my head. "Anna, the Fae and our mother are in our home with the children!" I all but screamed at her.

"I know, Olie, but we still haven't gotten what we came here for," she patiently reminded me.

I blew out a breath, willing my worry for my mate and family to simmer on the back burner for the moment. I never, ever, should have left him. I closed my eyes, pinching the bridge of my nose. Anna was right. I needed my denied magic. Without it, I would be no help in defending those I loved.

The bundle Ox was holding gave out an awful wail.

"She's hungry," Ox said, looking at Giv.

Giv shook his head. "The griffin is still out there."

My brow furrowed. "Where is her mother?"

Giv looked at me. "If what you say is true, that the Queen is your mother, then we are your brothers and that dying infant is your sister."

"She was left here to die?" I hissed.

Giv nodded. "We've been getting milk from the cows, but the griffins have moved in and we've already lost two brothers in order to feed her."

"Why didn't The Queen take you with her?" Anna asked.

"Our fathers are human, we provide no value to her," Ox shrugged, trying to quiet the screaming child.

My jaw locked and I dropped my bag. "How many griffins?" I asked.

"Olie," Anna tried.

"Three," Giv said. "They'll kill you."

I rolled my neck on my shoulder. This I could fix. "Once I kill them, get outside. I have no idea how to milk a cow."

"You draw them out, I'll guard one of them to milk the cow," Anna said, drawing a sword with a shrug. "We need to burn off some energy anyways."

I smiled at her. "Let's go kill shit."

We stormed to the door and I flung it open, not spending any time thinking about the fact we now had three additional relatives to feed or the toll it would take on the Magician and Amin to bring five people back over.

I stood in the open doorway a moment, taking in the hard-packed wine dirt.

"Be careful," Giv or Ox hissed behind us.

I ignored them, stepping out so Anna could slam the door behind me. Rotating my wrist to limber up my muscles, I scanned the area in front of me. The wooden barn was dark, but I could hear a distinct "moo." What the fuck were we going to feed the damn cow?

I squinted up into the maroon sky, searching for the winged assholes. I felt an itch growing between my shoulder blades.

Keeping my body rigidly still, I pulled my second sword. Pebbles fell behind me. I shifted my head to the left just a fraction of a centimeter, hoping to figure out how many were there. I filled my lungs, and on the exhale I turned, raising my swords and lowering my stance. Bring it, winged bitches.

On the flat roof, perched at the edge of the terra cotta wall, sat the winged beasts. I'm pretty sure those sharp beaks were smiling. Reason I need a flamethrower number one hundred and one: crispy birds would be efficient.

"Well, what do we have here?" the smallest one, on the far left, asked in a high-pitched timbre. She ruffled those sharp brown and white feathers, jumping down in front of me while I shifted back several steps. She was half the size of the one I had killed last time I was here. I wasn't foolish enough to think that meant she was an easier kill.

"Hi, I'm Olivia, here to kill you for starving an infant." I took a slow step backwards, wanting the fight to be away from the kitchen door to give Anna a chance to get the milk.

Bird brain followed me, ruffling her feathers again, squawking at me, snapping her beak close to my shin.

"They left us here!" she screeched. I winced, that was not a pleasant sound.

"Where did they all go?" I asked. I was really hoping her answer wasn't the same as Giv and Ox's.

She hopped, using her powerful feline back legs, easily cutting the distance between us in half. I shuffled back, watching her two companions drop down, stalking our progress. With a practiced movement, I stowed one blade, placing both hands on my first.

"HOME!" she screeched. "The Fae took them home."

Dammit. "Why?" I followed up quickly. I was trying not to make my usual mistake of killing before obtaining information. Look at that, I was making progress.

Her deadly feathers ruffled. "I don't know," she spat.

"You should. You've been trapped here for generations and unable to escape. Was there a failsafe this entire time?"

She snapped at me, wings partially extended as she tried to chomp me in half. I ducked under the chomping beak, barely. Swinging my sword wide, I aimed for her thick and scaly ankle. She yelled in outrage, but I didn't hear much pain in her scream, unfortunately.

"What are you?" she demanded.

I shrugged, "A woman on a mission."

"You look like her," she hissed, lunging at me again. I brought up my blade, ducking almost a second too late. Angling my blade into her chest, I pushed forward. My momentum was lacking, and while the sharpened steel found purchase, it wasn't a killing blow. My feet floundered, searching for traction in the rust dirt. I lunged, and with both hands wrapped painfully against the hilt, I pushed. My sword cleaved through bone, the loud popping giving way to soft tissue sliced under the pressure.

Now that was a scream of pain. Her beak snapped through the muscles of my shoulder with impressive speed.

With a surprised yell, I abandoned my blade, dropping flat to the ground and rolling away from the beak that followed me, slamming into the red earth. Fingers crossed she got stuck or I had hit something important.

I dodged her angry swipes, rolling, scooting and landing a solid kick against her front leg. Adrenalin dulled the pain in my shoulder. I needed to get back to that sword. The blade in her chest oozed with thick, black blood. At least that was a small victory, but it would mean nothing if I found death at her beak. Unlike my previous visit, I could die here this time around.

She angled me against another terra cotta structure and I pulled my second blade free with my good arm, staying low and breathing heavily. Sweat and dirt coating my open wound, I heaved a breath, watching her pursue me at her leisure. She lunged, tilting her head and opening her wound wide. I used the wall behind me, bracing a foot against it to give myself extra height and an angle to avoid the razor sharp edges of her beak.

My blade landed true between her shoulder blades, and my momentum embedded it deeply.

I recognized the death wail, her head thrown back as she bucked and tossed herself around in a desperate attempt to dislodge the blade. I kept my grip, not wanting to lose another needed weapon, adding my injured arm as my shoulder screamed at me.

Her body crumpled, legs folding in, eyes glazing over, before she fell heavily to the side. I pulled my bloody blade free, turning and coming face to face with another griffin. With a swift and efficient twist of its head, it sent me hurtling through the air and off its dead companion's body. I thumped in the red dirt with a groan, my blade spilling from my fingers.

In my brief aerial view, I had seen Anna fighting off the final griffin. Hopefully, Ox or Giv could get the milk now.

I had only seconds for those thoughts before I was rolling away from the stomping, clawed feet of the exceptionally pissed off griffin, intent on merging my body with the dusty red dirt beneath us.

Somehow in the dusty confusion of me rolling and changing directions to avoid his claws, I ended up directly underneath him—hence knowing that it was indeed a "him." I stopped rolling for a moment, pulling a dagger from my boot and throwing it at his dangling bits. A high-pitched scream met my successful throw, followed by the downward thrust of wings as he fled away from me.

Flopping to my stomach, I pulled my legs under me and pushed to a sitting position, breathing heavily. My shoulder throbbed in agony. I looked up, squinting against the blood red sun, watching the griffin turn in his flight, wings tucked close to his body, angling directly for me.

Shit. I stumbled up and ran for the carcass of the female griffin, grasping my blade in her chest and pulling at an awkward angle. The only saving grace was that her body shielded me as the second one slammed into her lifeless form.

The air was crushed from my lungs, my head smacking into the maroon ground. I wheezed, fingers searching for the blade I had freed moments before. I hissed trying to draw a breath, working my shoulders in an attempt to free myself. My progress was slow, my vision only of the wine sky. When the crushing weight disappeared, I wasted no time in surging upright and seeking my blades.

I brought the steel up just in time to slice through my attacker's beak.

"Whoa," I whispered, surprised. Not wasting the advantage, I thrust my blade between his shoulder blades, the scent of burning tickling my nose.

I stepped back, taking my blade with me as the griffin fell over, dead.

I looked down at my blade. The edges glowed scarlet and I knew it would be hot to the touch.

"A little help!" Anna yelled.

Turning, I saw her battling back the final griffin. Dark blood ran down various spots on his thick coat and face. She slashed, countering the slashing beak. I ran to her, holding my magical blade. I jumped, landing hard on the griffin's back and thrusting my blade down, carving the beast in the same manner as the second. He fell over without a sound.

I fell with him onto my side, my calf pinned underneath him, and painfully dragged myself away. Turning to sit on my ass, I saw the smoke drifting up from the wound, the edges of the feathers smoldering.

"How did you get a magic blade?" Anna asked, out of breath.

I shrugged. "I don't know. Their feathers the first time I was here were damn near impenetrable."

Anna held up her scratched arms. "I noticed."

I pushed up. "The baby fed?"

Anna nodded. "Get your sword."

She was right. Who knew what other surprises we were going to encounter. I cleaned the now cool blades the best I could before stowing them.

Ox walked out of the barn, his mouth hanging open, with a pail of milk.

"Let's go," I said to him, ushering him into the kitchen.

The baby was crying. Giv was standing. "I don't want it," he said.

Anna took the baby from him easily, cooing to her, I readied a bottle, handing it over to her.

"She's soiled," Anna said, not looking at me while she fed the tiny infant.

I nodded, rummaging through the cabinets, finding towels that I took down. "This will have to work until we get back home."

"I never thought I'd be happy to see a disposable diaper," she muttered.

I laughed, turning to Giv and Ox. "So, not fans of kids?"

Ox looked at Giv before shaking his head. "We've been jailed all our lives. This freedom and space is a little overwhelming."

I nodded. "Any chance you know where the library is?"

Giv shook his head. "After we found the baby, we stayed in the kitchen. We didn't know what else to do."

The baby now fed, Anna adjusted her hold and I helped her change the tiny one.

"She's so young," Anna said. "What's her name?"

They shrugged and I was annoyed I was related to such weaklings.

"She'd be perfect for Jerry and Mark," Anna whispered to me.

I stroked her soft cheek with a damp cloth, cleaning off the dirt there.

I laughed quietly, not wanting to wake her now that her tiny belly was full. "Think they can handle a half succubus baby?"

"I think it would be great fun to watch."

"You're taking the baby?" Ox asked.

"Yes. Prove that I can trust you, and I'll get you both out of here as well. We have an escape plan, but I have to find the books I was sent here for first."

They nodded, resolve slowly lifting their chins and stiffening their shoulders.

"What do we do with her?" Anna asked.

"Take her along for now. We don't know what other surprises are waiting for us."

She nodded.

...

We fashioned a sling for the baby, who needed a name, and gallivanted around the stone-walled palace searching for a massive hoard of books. Every door we opened was another disappointment.

I walked into my sixth, maybe seventh, room to find another dresser hanging open, clothing hanging out. I heaved a sigh. "Anything?" Anna asked.

"No, it's the same as the rest."

"We've got to be missing something. The only rooms we have entered have been living quarters. Aside from the kitchen, there should be an armory, library, laundry, bathing."

I sighed, turning and exiting the room. We had left Ox and Giv in the kitchen as they weren't much help. It would take work to rehabilitate them into society, and I didn't have time to start that at the moment.

"I think I can get us to the armory." I walked into the hallway, taking a moment to orient myself as to where The Magician's workroom was.

"I can take you to the armory," Ox said softly. Anna and I turned as one to see his form move away from the shadows.

"Lead the way," Anna said, her hands checking on the baby strapped to her while her eyes stayed squarely on Ox.

He nodded, walking slowly and casting watching glances behind to be sure we still followed. We twisted around to another wing of the palace.

Ox kept sending us discrete glances, once stopping to open his mouth before he closed it again and led on.

"What?" Anna finally asked, her clipped tone annoyed.

I gave her an equally annoyed look and she shrugged. "Clearly, he wants to ask us something."

"Yes, but he wasn't ready yet," I told her.

"Who has time for ready?"

"Whatever, Anna, your tact needs help, and trust me, that's saying a lot coming from me."

She huffed in agreement, well at least I was taking it as agreement.

"What is your world like?" Ox asked, the words spilling out quickly before he lost his nerve.

"Everything isn't red," Anna scoffed.

"We aren't governed by a Queen," I added. "Supernaturals are free to live their lives, so long as they don't harm humans."

That got Ox's attention. "Supernaturals don't harm humans?"

"Some do," I admitted, "but we try to take care of those quickly."

"Take care of?" Ox repeated, walking closer to us.

"Kill. We kill the Supernaturals who harm humans or other Supernaturals."

"Why?" Ox asked.

I raised my eyebrow. "Why do we kill them?" I asked, needing clarification.

Ox shook his head. "No, why do you protect Supernaturals?"

I shrugged, "Many aren't strong enough to do it for themselves."

Ox looked at me, his dark eyes searching my own. He was daring to hope, I recognized it. Daring to think of a life outside of pain and mere survival.

"How long were you locked up for?" Anna asked.

Ox shook his head. "Forty-two years."

"Wow, that makes our sixteen years seem pale in comparison," Anna commented. I nodded, agreeing. Forty-two years? He didn't look that old. No gray hair, no crow's feet, but didn't time move differently here? I swear The Magician had told me that.

"You two were slaves as well?" Ox asked, tentative hope infusing his voice, pushing his shoulders back for the first time.

"Yeah." Anna's voice was clipped.

"How did you escape?" Ox asked, entranced.

"We killed everyone," Anna said, moving around Ox to look down the hallway.

He indicated the hall to our left and Anna moved down it. Ox walked next to me.

"We were traded or sold to a vampire on Earth who trained us to be killers," I explained.

"Don't forget, she trained us to be whores as well," Anna called out.

I nodded. "She exploited our natural succubus abilities."

Ox nodded, clearly deep in thought, his brow furrowed. "But you escaped and have normal lives?"

Anna laughed, "Nothing about us is normal."

I shrugged as we came to the next junction, turning to face Ox. "Our past defines us. I kill to deal with it. Anna has her own coping mechanism, but yes, we have semi-normal lives."

Ox nodded before moving down another hallway.

"The food is way better on Earth," I continued on, trying to lighten the mood. "Let me tell you about pizza."

"Not to mention dessert," Anna added.

"One course at a time," I responded. We made lighthearted chatter about Earth for a bit until Ox finally stopped outside the armory.

Anna pushed open the iron gate with her foot. "Empty."

I looked over the barren shelves. "Clothing got left behind, weapons didn't."

"That doesn't bode well if they are on Earth," Anna stated, evidently feeling a need to point out the obvious.

"It does not," I agreed, my jaw clenched. I turned away. "Let's see what else is down this hallway, maybe we will get lucky and find the damn library."

"You said The Magician is going to be pulling you out of here?" Ox asked, walking next to me again.

"He should be. We had to solicit the help of a djinn, Amin, to help boost his magic. Once they are both recovered they will be opening a portal to get us out of here."

"Pending the djinn doesn't double cross you," Anna reminded me.

I sighed, "Yeah, I'm aware."

"How long?" Ox asked.

"A few days on the short end, a week on the long end."

Ox nodded thoughtfully. "I don't think we have food to survive that long."

"We have some provisions in our packs back in the kitchen. As long as the baby is fed, we can stretch our rations out," I told him.

He nodded and I turned to Anna, who was stopping in front of double doors.

"Will you stop leading with the child?" I hissed at her.

She huffed. "There has been nothing so far," she complained. Clearly the griffins didn't count in her estimation. Funny, though, my shoulder was still sore.

I gave her a pointed look, pulling my sword, and something crashed inside. I turned my attention from Anna to the closed doors in front of us.

"Stay here," I commanded.

"Oh, hell no. Here, take the baby," Anna said, carefully shifting the small bundle to Ox. He took her gently.

I rested my hand on the door, waiting until Anna was poised and ready. Together we each flung open a door, swords raised.

"Holy fuck," Anna whispered, taking a step back.

I steeled my nerves, not moving an inch. We had the baby to protect. Anna groaned, probably thinking the same thing as me.

I took a forced step forward and the door disappeared behind us.

"This isn't a good idea," she hissed right beside me.

"What we need is in here," I told her.

"You don't know that."

"Why else would they leave me behind?" a voice drifted down to us.

Anna and I stopped our forward movement into the humid jungle. Tall trees with thick leaves hung above our heads, our footfalls cushioned by lush ferns and overgrown grass.

"Who are you?" I asked, infusing my voice with confidence.

"I am Baqer, the God of Knowledge. Welcome to my humble home. I've been waiting for you, Olivia." Hearing him say my name with that kind of familiarity made me sick, helplessness washing over me for a moment before I trampled it back. We had just killed three griffins, we could figure out how to kill a Fae. Plus, I had a magical sword. Nothing to be scared of.

"Great, another fucking Fae who knows my name," I muttered.

"Hey, maybe keep this one alive to find out why this time," Anna added, always helpful.

I leveled her an annoyed glare before returning my gaze to the rainforest we had walked into. As I watched, the thick clouds above the canopy parted, and thousands of books nestled in cases lined the walls.

"We've come for The Magician's books. We don't want to hurt you." Again, I pushed confidence I didn't feel into my words.

The laughter from Baqer rang across the treetops, curling my stomach. Anna and I turned in unison, trying to follow the sound. I wasn't confident where it was coming from, and based on Anna's still-roving gaze, she wasn't, either.

"She said you would be confident. She forgot to mention foolish," Baqer taunted.

"Who?" Anna asked.

"Why, your mother, dear girl. She knew The Magician would be back, or rather he would send you back to obtain his books." That didn't feel like the truth, considering we hadn't even known I'd have to come back for his books. Unless it was all a careful ruse.

Maybe she knew The Magician and his magic better than I'd realized, or at least the spell that bound me.

"Ever get the feeling your dad isn't telling you everything?" Anna asked.

"All the time, but I need his help on this," I answered. "He wanted her brought back alive."

"Guess he got that wish," Anna muttered.

Guess he did.

We stood there for a few long moments, surveying our surroundings, waiting for Baqer to make a move. When he didn't, I called out, "So, you going to give me the texts or what?"

"Or what," came the answer. A short man hobbled out from the mist to our left.

Anna and I shifted to watch him push up the sleeve of his cobalt blue rob. He leaned heavily on a gnarled wooden staff, the pleasure he was drawing from this situation evident on his heavily wrinkled face.

"You have created quite a name for yourself, Olivia." I didn't like the way he said my name. It instantly made me feel dirty.

"How's that?"

"Oh, come now, ruler of The Council, Mate to the Alpha, and now here, trying to unlock your powers."

I regarded the short man silently. "No one was meant to have that much power," he stated, the serious tone running chills down my spine.

"According to who?" I demanded.

"Me, the Fae, the night. Does it really matter? All great empires fall." He pointed his staff at me. "And today is your demise."

"Technically, it's night," I pointed out.

Baqer thumped his staff against the mossy green undergrowth and the mist disappeared, revealing a large-paned window behind him. Another echoing slam of his staff, and the hues of red lightened to shades of yellow.

"To-day," he repeated.

"Well, ain't that fancy?" Anna muttered. "So what's the plan? Keep us here so The Queen can conquer Earth?"

Baqer sighed, an annoyed sound, before resting both twisted hands on top of his staff. "In laymen's terms, I suppose that would be correct, but it lacks the finesse and creativity we Fae are known for."

I'd have to agree; the fuckers were creative.

"So, you got the short straw being left behind?" I asked, playing a hunch.

His blue eyes burned with fire—literally, they ignited in white plumes. "I was selected to meet you for my exceptional skills."

I laughed, "I doubt that. If they really wanted me, they would have come and gotten me."

"Did you miss the Tree of Life visit?"

My eyes narrowed. "How did you know about that?" I asked.

Baqer smiled. Clearly, my interest was feeding his ego. The fire leaving his eyes, he bragged, "I know all."

"Bullshit," Anna called, twisting her wrist, loosening up the muscles.

Baqer snarled at her. With a flick of his staff, Anna's sword flew from her grasp.

"Shit," she hissed, drawing her other blade.

I fucking hated the Fae. They were far more powerful than me. I had no weapons that would last against him and his staff; my only hope was the magic bound inside of me. Maybe if I could touch him, I could fry him. I couldn't fail, too many were depending on me.

I really should have gotten that damn flamethrower already.

"How do we handle this?" Anna hissed.

"You die!" yelled Baqer.

"Not today," I yelled back, charging him. He shifted the point of his staff from Anna to me. The energy from the small man slammed into me. Instinctually, I brought my swords up to form an X, willing the metal protection properties it just didn't have.

To my surprise, it held. I looked up to see Anna's shocked face. "It's your guards," she began. Baqer didn't give her a chance to finish, blasting her surprised form with the same energy he had just unleashed on me.

With a yelp, she was flung into the tall trees.

I pulled my swords down, "I'm not sure what is going on, but I know I'm getting stronger. You should run."

I watched with dark glee as fear flicked across Baqer's features. "I fear no mortal."

I stepped closer to him. "I'm not so sure I'm mortal anymore."

I shouldn't have been able to cut through the griffin's feathers of steel as easily as I had. If Logan had evolved, it seemed I was doing the same.

Baqer's dark gaze roved over me, appraising. "You are bound, you pose no threat to me."

I shrugged, twirling my blades, a dark energy spreading down my limbs. It felt divine. A small voice of warning spoke up, but I ignored it. I needed the magic and the ability to kill the Fae.

Baqer's eyes narrowed and he muttered a word under his breath before slamming down his staff and tossing me back into the foliage.

I shouldn't have relaxed my grip on my swords. I let them go and flew into a wall of books, tumbling down into the thick trees.

"Fuck," I hissed, pushing up on all fours. I reached down and touched the abused flesh cut open on my side. With a groan I sat back on my heels, before standing up. I wasn't feeling so magical at this particular moment.

Maybe it was something to do with the swords. I needed them back, otherwise I had no idea if Anna and I would be getting out of there alive.

"Hey asshole!" Anna called out. I groaned, pushing away the ferns and thick, waxy leaves, rushing to find my blades before Anna got herself killed. I spied the silver of one instantly, snatching it up while I continued my search. I gave thought to hacking at the overwhelming greenery, but decided against it.

I heard her grunt followed by her annoyed scream, "Asshole!"

"Keep still, it has been some time since I've seen the offspring of The Queen," Baqer requested thoughtfully. He had to be kidding.

I shouldered the underbrush out of my way. One sword would have to be enough.

"Do you know who my father is?" Anna asked softly.

I stopped my approach. I knew this information was critical to Anna and I wasn't sure where else she was going to obtain it.

"You don't know?" Baqer questioned, surveying her, walking around her still form.

There was no guarantee that Baqer would tell her the truth, though. I debated, stepping forward quietly.

"No," Anna answered.

"Hmmm," Baqer mused. "Let me show you."

The jungle disappeared, along with my sword. I grunted, finding myself standing next to Anna.

"Is that me?" she asked softly.

I recognized the room as The Queen's chambers. I saw the bed with our mother in it. Her brow was slick with sweat, her cheeks pale as she held the small bundle of baby Anna to her breast.

"What are you going to do with her?" a voice asked The Queen. Anna and I turned as one to the man facing the large paned window, his back to us.

"Selena has offered me quite a sum for her," she said, a servant coming to take the babe. The Queen passed off Anna without regard for the infant's squawking.

"You should kill her." The man turned and I sucked in a breath. I'd recognize that evil face anywhere.

"Luharposn," I whispered. While a singular Fae had many faces, he enjoyed the skull of death best. I recognized the sharp cheekbones and soulless eyes that had spent lifetimes torturing me.

"Why kill her when she will fetch a price? Besides, the vampire will probably kill her, anyways." The Queen shrugged, the life of her child inconsequential.

"Now tell me, what of the other matter?"

The vision snapped out and we were standing in the nursery, in pristine condition with no broken window.

The nursery was cloaked in the dying red light from the bay windows, giving a pink cast to the normally pale skin tones of the father and infant daughter.

Gently, he stroked her face in the worn wooden rocker, cooing to her gently as she blinked large green eyes at him.

"You are so beautiful, little one," The Magician whispered to my infant self.

A delicate hand snuck out of her swaddle and tightly held onto his finger.

"So strong," he whispered, smiling down at me, his eyes brimming with tears. He took a shaky exhale, leaning back against the rocker as he held my small body tightly to his own.

I looked soft and warm wrapped up in the pale pink blanket. He knew he should put the baby down into the matching wooden crib carved with protective symbols, get some sleep before the ceremony tomorrow. He couldn't, he couldn't put his daughter down. How was he going to give her up tomorrow?

He felt the presence outside the door before the visitor knocked. "Enter," he called softly, allowing the wards to relax while Doyle's large body pushed through the double doors.

He stood almost to the ceiling, a minotaur of massive proportions, head of a bull with the body of an overgrown and exceptionally hairy man. The Magician could feel Doyle's dark gaze on him as the giant moved in front of him, kneeling down to place his large, horned head close to the child's.

"She is beautiful, Magician," Doyle commented.

"Thank you, Doyle."

Doyle lifted his dark eyes up, shifting his shaggy black head to stare into The Magician's eyes.

"You do not have to give her up," Doyle reminded him, reaching out a dark, hairy hand to stroke the girl's face.

"I don't have a choice in the matter," The Magician ground out through clenched teeth, involuntarily pulling his child closer to his chest.

"There is always a choice, Magician," Doyle claimed.

The Magician shook his head sadly, blinking back the tears.

"Shall I come back tomorrow?" Doyle asked softly.

"Yes," The Magician agreed, his eyes glued to the soft bundle in his arms.

Doyle lumbered his large body up, resting a furry hand on The Magician's shoulder. The Magician nodded once, relaxing the wards as Doyle exited.

Exhaling, The Magician continued to rock his daughter gently.

...

"What the fuck?" Anna yelled.

I shook my head, finding my equilibrium unbalanced after visiting first her birth story and then my own.

"Could you hear your father's thoughts?" I asked, slowly regaining awareness that I was indeed still holding my blade.

"He hates me," she spat. "That's the Fae who kept you prisoner when Selena double crossed them?"

I nodded, meeting her gaze. "Yes, he's a monster Anna, but he's an exceptionally powerful monster, which means..."

"I'm powerful, too."

I nodded. This was good, we were going to need a boost in power if we expected to defeat the library Fae.

Anna nodded back, her brow furrowed.

"I do so love the past, copious amounts of forgotten tidbits left lying around." Baqer strolled out through his mists again, his staff held tightly in his right hand; the Fae had a love of theatrics. "For instance, your father wanted to kill you," he said to Anna. "And yours gave you up even though he could have fought for you. The end result was the same, the rejects went to Selena."

Baqer shrugged as if our lives were no big deal. I grunted, my grip on my sword painful. The Fae walked over to Anna, lifting a short red lock. I tried to move, but found myself immobilized yet again. Dammit! I was painfully close to Anna.

"It's fascinating to me that both your fathers bound your inherited magic—perhaps so you couldn't kill them later? It is quite the quandary, as though they had knowledge of future events," the asshole mused.

"Those are big fucking words for such a small asshole," I taunted. I wasn't about to admit that he was probably right. The Magician had said I was the key to his freedom more than once. It left me feeling sickly used.

His eyes narrowed, the fire back in them, "You will do well to respect me. I have full permission to do whatever I please with you both."

"No," Anna said, "you don't."

She snatched the sword from my hand and I willed my fingers to let go. She swung it across Baqer's smug face. His mouth opened in shock as the blade cut him into two pieces.

The illusion of the forest fell away, replaced by just a library.

Anna heaved several breaths as the body of the Fae shriveled into itself until nothing was left.

"Do you think he is really dead?" Anna asked, her voice soft as she looked down upon the brown residue Baqer had left behind.

"I hope so. I don't think he would play dead. He had permission to do what he wanted," I told her, coming to stand by her side.

Anna nodded, and I knew the memory Baqer had shown her was eating her alive. My father might be an asshole who sold me, but at least he had, in some twisted way, loved me.

"Who do you think grants that permission?" Anna asked, turning to me and handing me my blade.

"My guess would be the Fae Queen. Our mother doesn't hold that kind of rank or power over the Fae."

"Do you think she is the one who took our mother to Earth?"

I shrugged, going to pick up my other blade. "I don't know, but let's see if we can find the books we need."

Anna nodded, going to the door and letting Ox and the infant in.

"What took so long?" he asked, looking around the dusty library.

"Fae problems," Anna muttered, not expanding on the matter.

Ox nodded, looking around the library. "You remember the titles?" I asked Anna.

"Yes. Ox, do you want the list of titles as well to help search?" Anna asked, approaching a shelf.

Ox shook his head. "We were never taught how to read," he admitted.

"See, Olivia, maybe there are benefits to being sold to an insane vampire," Anna chided me.

I grunted, refusing to agree to that statement.

"At least they didn't kill us," Anna commented under her breath.

I sighed, pausing in my perusal of the leather-bound texts in front of me, turning to watch Anna across the room.

"Our past does not define us, Anna. Our choices today do."

It was her turn to grunt at me. I turned back to the books. She had to let it go, not that I was entirely successful in following my own advice.

Chapter 5

Logan rubbed his temples. "What do you mean, 'We have a problem?'" he grumbled at Jerry.

"They're not waking up. Amin is a djinn, he shouldn't be unconscious, not for this long," Jerry said, sitting across from Logan in the office.

Logan drummed his thick fingers on his oak desk. It was his third desk. He and Olivia had broken the first two, and he was about to crush this one as well.

"What are our options?"

Jerry shrugged, shaking his head. "Hope Olie figures it out."

Logan leaned back forcefully in his chair. "That's not good enough."

Jerry shrugged, meeting his gaze. "It's not like we have a coven at our disposal. Olie killed off one of the most powerful, and the others are not exactly lining up to help us."

Logan continued to drum his fingers. "What about the necromancer?"

Jerry blinked at him. "Jaelle?" he said after a pause, finally remembering the name of the necromancer Olivia had saved. After, of course, being kidnapped along with Mark and Jerry.

Logan nodded. Jerry sat back in his seat, crossing his arms over his lean chest. "I don't know if she can help, or if she'd be willing."

Logan grunted, "Find out if she can. I'll handle the willingness."

...

We loaded the books requested by my father to the kitchen.

"Where is Giv?" Anna asked, using the metal pail to fill another bottle for the baby.

"I don't know," Ox answered, opening the door to look outside. "The cow is gone," he commented.

"What?!" I asked, going to stand next to him before pushing outside. The dead griffin carcasses still sprawled in the red dirt, but there was no cow.

"Anna," I said, turning back. She came to the doorway, shaking her head.

"Our packs are gone," she reported.

"Fuck," I hissed. "Where the hell could he have gone?"

"Does it matter?" Anna sighed. "We only have maybe another day's worth of milk for the baby. We don't have time to hunt him down and bring back the cow. Not to mention that we can't separate in case your father calls you back early."

"Dammit." I wanted to hunt Giv down and slit his throat, family or not.

"Is she going to die?" Ox asked, looking down at the small bundle in Anna's arms.

"No." I stormed over to the dead griffin bodies, pulling off a handful of feathers, ignoring the pain in my palm.

I stood, seeing Anna and Ox watching me. "We are going to open a portal on this side."

Anna moved back as I marched in and dropped my handful of feathers on the butcher block counter.

"How?" Ox asked, stunned.

"I'm the daughter of a Magician. Anna is the daughter of a Fae. We have the power, we just need the knowledge." Anna met my gaze before turning to study the books resting on the counter.

"Let's get to work," she said, handing the baby to Ox.

"Ox, let's teach you the alphabet while we work." I tore a blank piece of paper from one of the books before I went to the hearth and pulled out a piece of charcoal.

Ox looked up at me, surprised, then lowered his eyes to the page, watching my drawings intently.

"You get to sing, Anna," I told her, laughing.

"I don't sing." She glared at me before reciting the ABCs for Ox.

I easily found the spell my father had used. I remembered the ingredients: griffin feathers, unicorn horn, and shadow lark.

"Did you find it?" Anna asked, coming to stand next to me.

"I did."

"What's wrong?"

"It took me a week to gather the shadow lark and unicorn horn. The last two ingredients I wasn't conscious enough to even know how to obtain." I looked at Anna. "We don't have that kind of time."

"Maybe there is another spell," she offered, opening another leather-bound text and flipping through the pages.

I nodded, not voicing the hopelessness waiting to be unleashed. It would do us no good.

Tommy typed rapidly on Logan's desktop computer, grumbling. "I don't know why you can't have this conversation in my room."

Logan raised an eyebrow at him. "You have a half-naked woman in the poster across from your desk."

"That's She-Ra, and she's a bad ass," Tommy corrected him.

Logan leaned back in his high-backed office chair. "Not the message I am looking to send."

Tommy shrugged, slowing down as he typed the last few keystrokes. "Alright, hit enter and you are ready to go." He went to sit next to Jerry, while Mark relaxed on the couch.

Logan looked over the trio, knowing none of them would be leaving. They wanted Olie back; at least this time, she hadn't been shot.

He cleared his throat and hit enter.

Jaelle's sleepy face came on the screen, her pale head propped in her hand.

Logan cleared his throat again. Jaelle jumped before rubbing her eyes. "Logan," she greeted him. "You have some of the best hackers in the world. I never dreamed to be found by you, nor did I think commandeering my phone in such a way was possible."

Logan gave her a half smile. Tommy had harangued her for close to an hour before she relented and agreed to take the Alpha's call.

"We need you and your coven to come to St. Ann. We need your help."

Jaelle leaned back in her chair, crossing her arms over her frail body. "You have your own mage, besides I'm not even stateside."

"He isn't powerful enough on his own for what needs to be done," Logan admitted. He certainly didn't enjoy admitting a weakness, his own or anyone else's.

Jaelle continued to watch Logan intently. "You haven't yet told me what this is about."

"Nor do I plan to," Logan answered.

Jaelle sighed. "I owe Olivia, not you. Have her call me." She hit a button on the computer to end the call.

Tommy laughed.

"What the hell!" Jaelle yelled, smashing her computer in frustration.

"She can't hang up," Tommy chuckled.

Logan moved closer to the computer screen. "Jaelle, you have two hours to get to the mansion, or I'm coming for you."

Tommy reached over and hit a few buttons, ending the call.

"I assumed you were done," Tommy said.

"I was." Logan leaned back, steepling his hands.

"What now?" Jerry asked.

"I hacked into the security cameras at the hotel in Mexico where Jaelle is staying. I'll know when she checks out," Tommy said, dashing from the room.

"You think she will do what you said?" Mark asked from the couch.

Logan rubbed his forehead. "I'm open to other ideas."

"Let us take the jet to where Jaelle and her coven are, and escort them back," Mark said.

Logan nodded. "Do it."

...

I was re-reading the spell I had found when Anna came to stand over my shoulder.

"Absolutely not," she said, trying to pull the book away from me.

"Look Anna, it says to drain a succubus or incubus, which none of us are, but what if we take a little from each of us?"

I looked over at Ox, seeing him watching us closely, his mouth hanging open. "Would you be willing to contribute?" I asked him.

He nodded before looking down at the baby. "We wouldn't take any from her," Anna said quickly.

Ox nodded. "This will get us out of here?"

"Hopefully. It's our best option. I think we can find the rest of the supplies here so we don't have to waste time on traveling," I answered.

"If it doesn't work?" Ox asked, shifting in his seat.

"Then we try something else, until we find a way out of here." I stood up, placing a hand on Ox's shoulder. "We don't give up, ever."

Anna grunted, and I raised an eyebrow at her. "Let's go storm the castle," she smiled.

I nodded, about to head to my father's study when the ground began to rumble.

"What the fuck?" Anna and I asked in unison, moving to the kitchen door.

Ox stayed at the island, holding the child close.

"Don't come out until we tell you," I told him, moving to the door and stepping outside.

Anna and I turned to the right, watching the cloud of dust billowing our way.

"Any idea what it is?" she asked me out of the side of her mouth.

I shook my head. We drew our swords in unison.

"No time like the present to find out," I grunted. Nothing was getting past us. Anna and I held our stances tensely while the dust cloud pounded closer.

I squinted into the thick red dust. "What the fuck?" I whispered.

From the brief glances of brilliant purples, iridescent blues, and pearl whites, my mind pieced it together. "It's the unicorns," I said, dropping my stance and stowing my blade.

Anna glanced at me before turning her attention to the slowing dust.

"You certain?" she asked.

"No," I answered honestly.

"Dammit, Olivia," she hissed at me, stowing her blade. "You better be fucking right about this."

The ground stopped rumbling as the horses slowed to a trot. "Unicorns," Anna breathed, squinting and coughing out the dust.

"Unicorns," I agreed, without the wonder. "I don't remember them having riders," I mused.

A pearl white horse stepped forward with an obsidian horn. On his back rode a dark-haired beauty.

"They friends?" Anna asked.

I shrugged, "Hopefully." The woman slid from the unicorn's back.

"Olivia, daughter of The Queen and The Magician, have you come to pay your debts?" she asked.

"That depends, any chance you have a spare horn and a shadow lark with you?" I asked.

The pearl unicorn stomped his feet. "You have already taken from us! How dare you demand more?"

I narrowed my eyes at him. "Watch it, or I will leave you here to rot."

He scoffed, "You are the daughter of the liar. I shouldn't be surprised that you continue that legacy."

"Hey, any chance anyone saw a skinny asshole with a cow?" Anna asked.

The unicorn dropped his head to Anna. "Why?"

"We need the cow," Anna said, his proximity not fazing her.

"They didn't make it past the snake pit," the unicorn shook its head.

"Fuck," I hissed.

"Why did you need the cow?"

The door to the kitchen opened, the baby wailing. "I think she's hungry," Ox said. "We don't have any more food."

"Dammit." I turned to him, but the mermaid stopped me.

"That is what you needed the cow for?" she asked me.

I nodded.

"We can help, one of our sisters is nursing a child."

"Good, we don't have much time. The Queen and all her court are on Earth. I have to get back to protect ... well, basically everybody," I said. "Now, about those items."

...

Mark, Jerry, and Jaelle's entire coven had landed thirty minutes earlier and been shuttled over to the mansion. Everyone was assembled in the backyard. Jaelle claimed the outdoors quieted them after such a traumatic, forced journey.

"Olivia is trapped in the red world. Her father, The Magician, and a djinn sent her through to gather information, but neither of them has regained consciousness," Logan explained.

Jaelle shook her head, the coven wandering around her restlessly. They made Logan nervous; he could scent the stench of death on them.

"We know nothing of other realms," Jaelle said, rattling the thin bracelets on her wrists. "Had you just explained the situation, it would have saved us both time."

Logan growled and Jaelle stepped back.

"Can you help wake up The Magician and the djinn?" Logan asked.

Jaelle shrugged. "We deal in death, not healing."

"Is there something buried here?" one of the necromancers asked, kicking a clump of dirt.

Logan raised his eyebrows. "Not that I know of."

"What are you sensing, Dacey?"

The young girl shrugged her thin shoulders, her fingers flexing at her sides. "I don't know, something."

"What guarantees do we have?" the large unicorn named Hemit rumbled.

"None, except that I am as anxious to get out of here as you are," I told him honestly.

He grumbled before lowering his head. "Take it, before I change my mind."

I reached up, slightly freaked out as I tugged the thick-based black horn free from his face. It came away easily, revealing a skinnier horn underneath.

"Cool," Anna breathed.

I handed her the horn, before turning to the river-eyed mermaid named Arista. "So, you have legs."

"We do," she agreed.

"Look, I was going to come back, I actually have properties already for the unicorns." Hemit huffed behind me. I got the feeling he didn't believe me.

"How did your mother leave?"

"The fucking Fae," I hissed.

Arista nodded, "And what about us?"

I shrugged. "We've had issues. I haven't had time to scout for properties."

Arista shook her head. "The shadow lark is pure energy, what was taken hasn't regrown yet.

"Shit," I grunted, turning away from her. Blood spell it was, then.

"But, we can give you a boost."

I groaned, "That's going to fucking hurt."

"What about the other items, Olivia?" Ox asked, watching everything nervously.

"We can try merging the two spells, use our blood to make up for the missing ingredients," Anna offered with a shrug.

I groaned, shrugging my own shoulders in return. "Sure, what the fuck do we have to lose?"

...

Dacey knelt in the wet grass, using her hands to pull back the earth. "Something is here, but not," she mused.

The others gathered around her in their frail, unnerving ways.

Jerry squinted at the spot Dacey was working on. "She's right," he confirmed.

Jaelle turned to him, surprised.

...

"Alright big boy, smash those," Anna said, setting his horn and the griffin feathers under Hemit's hooves.

He looked at her from black eyes and I could only imagine what we wanted to tell her. Anna shrugged, waving her hand in a get-to-it fashion.

Hemit huffed, obliging her.

I turned to Arista, holding out my hand. She had pulled from each of her fellow mermaids and was glowing. "Are you ready, Olivia?"

"Ready as I'll ever be," I grunted as her hand clamped down on my own.

I groaned, my body arching forward, a scream clamped between my grinding jaws as pure white energy shot up my arm. Don't ask me how I knew the color when my eyes were closed, but I felt the searing heat and wished for the cool waters of the muddy-banked river.

I straightened up, finding myself able to release Arista's hand before I leaned over, resting my hands on my thighs.

"The babe won't take my milk," a voice said, with wailing following on its heels.

I grunted, blinking back white spots and forcing the pain in my head to manageable levels.

"Hemit done?" I asked, turning to Anna.

The unicorns were watching me intently.

"Yep, all dust," Anna said, bending down to pick it up.

"Leave it," I commanded, shaking my head.

Anna looked up at me. "We need rope, quickly," I rasped at her.

Anna nodded, heading into the barn and producing what I needed.

"Hemit, you are going in first, with Ox and the baby tied to you," I commanded.

He huffed, "I will not ride with a halfling."

I snarled, the sound ripped from my very soul, turning on him. He backed up quickly. "You will do as I say or you will rot here."

I didn't recognize my voice.

"Easy Olie, it's the magic. Your eyes are black," Anna counseled me.

I nodded, drawing an anger-infused breath before turning back to Hemit. He knelt down and I nodded.

Ox handed the baby to me before awkwardly mounting Hemit's back. I looked down on the soft, malnourished bundle. "Hang on, beautiful, we are going to get you help," I whispered, kissing her forehead.

"Use the sling to tie her to you, be sure the rope doesn't cut into her." Ox nodded, silently accepting the rope. Anna moved to help him.

I blew out a breath and wrapped the books in a curtain. Handing them to Arista, I warned, "These have to make it through. I have to be able to defeat my mother before she makes Earth like this place."

Arista nodded, "I accept the charge."

"Alright, let's do this." I had read the spell over fifty times already. I lacked the love potion from my mother and the dust of the high desert, but I had plenty of dirt and here's hoping blood as well.

Slicing my wrist open with a dagger, I let the bright crimson pool onto the crushed horn and griffin feathers.

"Do you want mine as well?" Anna asked.

I nodded, pumping my hand to get more blood to flow. She knelt next to me, slicing her own wrist.

"Any special words?" she asked after we had both stopped.

I exhaled, laying my hand on the blood and dust, pushing the borrowed mermaid energy into the pile. Everything snapped into high-definition clarity.

"By my blood, by my oath, by my right, open the portal to where my bones call home." I imagined the backyard of the mansion, where Logan's well loved and falling apart grill had been placed. The pool where Tommy loved to play water basketball. The grass Ginny so often would climb off her blanket to pull at and try to eat.

The ground in front of us yawned open and Anna fell through with a scream. I pushed back, the portal following me, eating at the ground.

"GO! GO! GO!" I screamed. Mermaids and unicorns both flew by me. The portal called me, demanded me. I wanted to go through, needed to.

My body moved forward, but I forced myself back with a groan. Bodies flew by me, and I bowed my head. With a scream, the last went through and I let the portal take me, the anticipation of Logan's arms and soft grass a whispered promise.

...

Logan didn't understand a word the necromancers were chanting, but Jerry was sitting cross-legged with them on the ground, listening to something Logan couldn't hear.

Logan shifted his weight, crossing his arms over his chest. Mark stood next to him, sharing in his discomfort.

The ground rumbled, and they were both rocked back.

"Get out of there!" Logan yelled, his voice lost as a huge portal opened in the center of the circle. There wasn't time; the wind howled, whipping around them. Huge horses tumbled out, tossed around like rag dolls. Only one stood its ground and Logan turned, not believing his eyes.

A pure white unicorn with an obsidian horn carried a man clutching a makeshift sling to his chest, while a rope dug into his waist.

Logan recognized that sling style, it was something Olie used to cart Ginny around in. Partially shifted, he was moving toward the man before he even realized it, slicing through the ropes with his claws and helping the man down.

"The baby—she needs—she needs food," the man whispered before losing consciousness.

Logan turned, seeing Tommy in the doorway at the back of the house. "Get formula, now!!" He screamed.

Tommy stood shell-shocked for only a moment before he was moving.

Logan turned to the portal. "Olivia," he whispered, as bodies kept being tossed around. There was a pause and then the portal shuttered before drawing in on itself.

"NO!" Logan bellowed.

...

I groaned, curled up on my side, my head splitting with pain, my body feeling skinned alive. I didn't even care that grass had been shoved into my mouth.

"Yuck," I coughed, spitting out the moist dirt. Hell, at least it wasn't red. I rolled to my back, looking up at the beautiful, dark night sky.

A caramel head came into my view and I smiled. "Hey honey, I'm home," I croaked.

Logan smiled, dropping to his knees and pulling me into his arms. I groaned in contentment. "And you brought friends," he murmured.

I laughed, "Yeah, yeah, I did."

Chapter 6

I took Logan's offered hand as I stood up, the vertigo causing me to sway slightly. Once my vision stopped swimming, I looked around the backyard. Unicorns pawed the fresh dirt, jumping and bucking in joy. The mermaids had taken to the pool, jumping in and laughing. I couldn't help but smile, freedom was always something to celebrate.

Anna rolled into a sitting position, spitting out grass with a groan.

"What the fuck?" she asked, standing up, arms braced wide as she stumbled.

Hemit shook his head, prancing with his pack. "The baby?" I asked with urgency.

Logan turned me. There, sitting on a deck chair, was Tommy, feeding the baby and talking to Ox, like all this was normal. New babies, new faces, new races. I shook my head, instantly regretting it as I swayed again. Maybe this was our normal. This band of outsiders I claimed as my own.

"One problem down," I muttered. "What is Jaelle doing here?"

"Your father and Amin are unconscious. We needed the coven to reach you." Logan tightened his arm around my shoulders. I sagged into him.

I nodded, heaving a sigh. The only thing I wanted to do was rest in Logan's warm and never-failing embrace.

"How long have I been gone from here?" I asked him, pulling back and standing on my own. He hesitated to release me, but I had to appear strong here, had to set the right tone for everyone: This bitch could spin spells, open a portal and still kick ass.

Logan chuckled, clearly having heard that mental pep talk.

"Three days," he answered.

"It was only a day for us," I told him. I needed to tell him everything that had happened, the memories of my father and Anna's father. I needed him to help me sort through the new and conflicting emotions I was having about The Magician.

I groaned, exhaling a breath before pushing all that mess back down where it belonged.

We had work to do.

I turned to see Mark helping Jerry up.

Jaelle had regained her footing and was checking on her coven. I moved toward her. Sensing my approach, she straightened her pearl white robes, brushing off flecks of dirt.

"Quite an entrance," she began.

I shrugged. "The usual. How did you know where I would be?"

"Dacey sensed something," she said, nodding to a young member righting herself.

"Nice work, Dacey," I told her. She smiled timidly, shrugging.

Mark finished righting Jerry, helping him over to us.

"About damn time, Olie," Jerry grunted.

"Wasn't even a full day where I was," I informed him.

"Whatever, how did you get back?" he asked.

"Magic, luck, and blood."

Jerry nodded. "I think you pulled from us as well."

I nodded, rubbing the back of my neck, a throbbing building at my temples.

"Hey, so I've solved your adoption issues. Go see Tommy, that's my half-sister."

Logan grunted, looking down at me. "A little more finesse in informing them they are about to be parents to your own blood might have helped."

I shrugged, turning to see the shocked faces of Jerry and Mark. They were both still, hardly breathing and ashen faced.

So I could see Logan's point, but I didn't have the time.

"Come on," I said to them, moving to Tommy and Ox, who had made it into a sitting position, resting his thin arms on his knees, looking around in wonder.

"We have a new baby?" Tommy asked, holding the baby bottle like a professional.

"Mark and Jerry are going to raise her," I explained. "If they want to," I added.

I turned to see Jerry reaching out tentatively to the small bundle.

Tommy looked at me, confused. I nodded and he handed over the baby with the bottle.

"She's really hungry," Tommy said.

"Our mother left her, abandoned her," Anna informed him, venom dripping from her words.

I looked over at her. She was worn, her steps heavy and slow. I wasn't the only one hurting from losing blood creating the portal and energy passing through it. But none of that compared to the memory she had seen.

I rested a hand on her shoulder. "We will find her."

"Find who?" Logan asked.

I sighed. "Our mother wasn't in the red world. In fact, only Ox and the baby were left behind there." No need to mention Giv, he'd gotten what he deserved. "We found a Fae in the library and learned that Mommy Bitchest had brokered a deal with the Fae for passage here."

Logan nodded, the relief and happiness over my return draining away.

Mark looked down over Jerry's shoulder at the little infant. At least something good was coming of this.

"Why can't we keep her?" Tommy asked, looking back at them.

I rested a hand on his shoulder. "She has a chance at a normal life, untainted by our tortured pasts. Let her have that. Besides, it's not like she won't be over all the time."

"She is our sister," Anna said with a smile.

"What's her name?" Mark asked, looking up at me with tears in his eyes.

I shook my head. "She doesn't have one."

Mark nodded, looking back down at the baby.

"What of me?" Ox asked softly.

I sighed. "We will get you a room set up. I'll have to figure out a tutor to get you up to speed." Placing a hand on his shoulder, I added, "But you are safe now. No one will harm you. No one will force you to do anything against your will." He met my sincere gaze with hardly restrained tears.

"Thank you, sister," he whispered.

I nodded before standing.

"Let's go see my father. I'm going to need him awake to figure out where my mother is."

"Where are the books?" Anna asked, searching the ground and finally spotting them. "I'll grab them, you see your father."

I nodded, heading inside, noting the sadness in her voice.

"What happened?" Logan asked, keeping pace with me. I felt Tommy following closely.

"The Fae we killed showed us memories of our fathers. Anna's is Luharposn, and he wanted her killed at birth. She's taking it hard."

"What of your father?" Logan asked.

I sighed, turning to face him at my father's doorway. "He loved me, and had a hell of a time giving me up. After seeing how Ox was treated, I'm understanding more why he did what he did."

Logan nodded and I opened the door before we could get further into the complex emotions that were clouding my ironclad disgust with my father.

Doyle raised his back and silver fur-covered head in the small room, a single lamp throwing more shadows than light. "You have returned," he announced with no joy.

"You don't sound surprised," I said to him, moving into the room, crossing my arms over my chest.

Doyle shrugged, "You are his daughter, you share his stubbornness and intelligence."

I couldn't argue with that, going to my father's bedside. "Why hasn't he woken up yet?" I asked.

Doyle shifted nervously. "It is too early for him to wake after such an exhausting feat. The real question is, why hasn't Amin woken up?"

I turned to Doyle. "The Queen is here."

Doyle nodded his head solemnly. "I have been pondering the meaning of the spirit tree. Her arrival would be an appropriate explanation."

"Any idea how to find her?" I asked.

Doyle shook his head. "She had powerful allies help her over, they will keep her safe."

I grunted. "What can we do to wake him up faster?"

"Have you recovered your power?"

"No," I admitted reluctantly. I'd have loved for the wall inside of me to come crashing down, but that wasn't happening.

Doyle nodded, turning his attention back to the prone form of my father. "You obtained the books."

Again, it wasn't so much a question as a statement. "We did."

"Your answer is there. Once you have your power, there will not be many things you cannot do."

He was being cryptic, but at least he was helping. I looked down at my father. I had envisioned him guiding me along this path, but maybe I had to walk it alone.

I nodded, bundling down my emotions and renewing my guards, then standing. "I better see to Amin."

We left the room, with Logan leading the way to the spare guest room in the basement. Amin was in the same shape as my father, unresponsive.

"Jerry thinks something went wrong that they are both unconscious."

"It's possible. It would have been smart of my mother to leave a booby trap, if one can booby trap a portal." I sighed, rubbing my head.

"You need to rest," Logan counseled me.

I nodded. "But I need to eat first."

...

I checked on the mermaids and unicorns, finding them content in the backyard. Mark and Jerry were giving the baby a bath and using some of Ginny's old clothing to dress her.

Satisfied that I could relent in controlling for a while, I plunked down at the farm style kitchen table to be fed.

As Logan dropped another grilled cheese in front of me, I told him yet again, "I hate that red world."

"Hopefully, there will never be a reason to go back."

I grunted in agreement as Anna sat down across from me, looking weary. The exhaustion was settling into my own bones as well.

"What's next?" Anna asked, no more in shape than I was to actually do anything.

I rubbed my eyes, fighting back a yawn. "We need to unlock my power, and hope that I can figure out a way to wake up my father."

Anna nodded, "To kill my father."

I shifted in my seat, meeting her gaze intently. "If he is here and I can, I will."

Anna nodded but set her jaw firmly. "He's mine, Olivia."

I nodded. "Alright. We need to figure out what powers you have as well."

"Tomorrow," Logan said firmly, pulling me up.

Anna sighed, "Yeah, I don't suppose we are much good to anyone like this."

89

"The mermaids and unicorns—" Anna and I began.

"Ali, Grant and Hudson will handle it," Logan scolded, pushing me up the stairs. "Do not make me come back for you as well, Anna," he said without turning around.

I laughed, hearing her grumbling as her chair scraped against the tile. My legs were heavy as I stomped up the stairs.

"No, I will not carry you," Logan grumbled behind me. I gave a half-hearted attempt at a laugh, turning down the hallway and pushing into our bedroom with a grunt.

The moment the door closed behind us, Logan's hands were on me, holding me, protecting me. He heaved a deep sigh. "I thought I'd lost you again," he whispered.

"Come on, Logan," I mumbled into his chest. "Nothing can come between us. Nothing is strong enough to divide us, not in this life or the next."

Whoa, that was a little deep for me. I ignored his shocked look and pushed him into the bathroom. "Let's go, I need to heal."

He smiled, tugging at my clothing, his lips crushing mine.

Chapter 7

Lying on my side, I watched Logan sleep on his back, a tan arm over his stomach, his other hand resting on my arm. We had fallen asleep facing each other only a few short hours ago.

Our short but immensely enjoyable lovemaking in the shower had helped recharge me, but I found myself burdened by everything that had happened.

My father was unconscious, Amin as well. Our backyard was overwhelmed by magical creatures. I rolled to my back with a sigh.

I needed to look at the texts we'd brought back. I debated for a moment how pissed Logan was going to be, but I wasn't sleeping, no sense in wasting valuable time.

Carefully, I eased myself out of the bed and dressed in my trademark yoga pants and tank top.

Padding down the stairs, I listened to the quiet of the early morning in the mansion. In the kitchen, I poured a bowl of cereal and a cup of coffee. I know, we are all shocked I can use a coffee maker. It wasn't long before I had company.

Anna grunted a hello, pouring her own coffee but not seeking food.

We sat for a few moments in silence. I rinsed my bowl, setting it into the dishwasher. Coming to stand in front of Anna, I met her intense gaze, an immeasurable history of pain between us.

I nodded. We were driven by our demons. I didn't need to have a conversation about taking it easy or healing. I certainly didn't want to hear that speech from her.

"Books?" I asked.

"Books," she agreed, taking her coffee and slipping off the barstool.

"Where are they?" I asked.

"Library," Anna informed me, taking another sip of her coffee.

I nodded, heading to the expansive library. We had updated it upon moving in with numerous electrical outlets, comfortable couches, and built-in shelving. Oddly enough, I had collected a substantial number of texts in my short life of freedom. I suppose with a horde of children being educated at the mansion, it wasn't that surprising.

The books in question had been set upon the sturdy wooden table. Anna and I took seats opposite each other, each pulling out one of the books.

"So, what are we looking for, exactly?" Anna asked.

"I don't know," I confessed. "Something that will break the hold on my magic or that will help heal The Magician."

"Or kill a Fae," Anna muttered under her breath.

I grunted, "Yeah, that would be perfect."

"Why does it always fall to us to fix everything?" Anna grumbled.

"Because we can," I answered, turning over the ancient pages slowly. "Because we have important people to protect."

Anna sighed. "Life would be easier in a log cabin with no one around."

"Easier," I agreed, "but lonely."

"No worse than the damn isolation tank," Anna grumbled.

I slammed my book closed. "Why the fuck would you bring that shit up?"

My outburst caught her off guard. She pulled back from her book, blinking up at me with crystal blue eyes.

"How can you not think about it? How can you not wonder if it would be easier to be dead?"

I breathed heavily, watching her, debating how to answer. I might have thought those things, but I never gave them voice.

"We survived, Anna, against all odds. That has to mean we were destined for something more than being some fucked up vampire's pets."

Anna cleared her throat and nodded, not meeting my pointed gaze. I couldn't fix her. Hell, I couldn't fix myself. All I could do was point us at our next target and hope that killing shit would once again help ease the guilt and memories.

"No Logan?" Anna asked. I opened the book back up.

"No, unlike us, he sleeps," I answered.

"He snores," Anna said with a sly smile.

"How do you know that?" I asked, turning my full attention to her.

"He fell asleep on the couch."

I laughed, "Yeah, he does snore."

"Does it bother him that you can't have children?" Anna asked, turning a page.

I looked up at her, my turn to be surprised. "He's never acted like it mattered, nor have I gotten any feelings about it through the bond," I answered with a shrug. "But it may at some point when life settles down and Ginny isn't the baby anymore. He loves her, but I'm not sure one is enough for him."

"At least he has her," Anna tried.

I nodded, staring down blankly at the pages in front of me, painfully aware of what I could never give Logan and what Lorraine had.

Page after page, I understood less and less. The spells were complex, the ingredients unknown. Who keeps a hex bag blessed in the blood of a bone broth handy? And what the fuck did that even mean?"

I sat back in my chair with a defeated grunt. "I don't understand anything."

Anna sighed. "Me, either. The words are English, but put together as they are, they make no damn sense."

"Did the necromancers stay?" I wondered aloud.

Anna shrugged. "I don't know. Haven't checked."

I nodded, standing up. "I'm going to check on Amin and my father, you handle the backyard?"

Anna nodded. "Mermaids and unicorns, who would have thought?" she mumbled.

Not me.

I went upstairs and into the second wing, knocking softly on my father's door. I heard Doyle moving behind the door before he opened it.

"Olivia," he greeted me, nodding deeply.

"Doyle, have you slept?" I asked, worried about the drooping shoulders of the minotaur.

"No," came his curt reply as he heaved his massive weight down into the same chair as before.

I sighed, going to sit next to my father. His condition hadn't improved; in fact, in only a few hours, he looked worse.

The skin under his eyes was sunken, his tone ashen. I ground my jaw, hating how useless I was in this situation.

"Has Amin woken up?" I asked, keeping my eyes upon my oblivious father.

"No."

I turned to Doyle. "I'm running out of options, Doyle. Do you know of anything that might help him wake up?"

Doyle shook his head. "I am only a guardian."

I nodded, rubbing my head. "I'm going to check on Amin." I stood wearily.

"Logan had him moved into the next room," Doyle informed me, his gaze not leaving my father. I nodded. While he might claim to be my guardian, he was my father's first, without a doubt.

I opened the next door, seeing the lamp next to the bed turned on. I padded softly into the room, looking down at Amin. While he didn't look as close to death as my father, his complexion had lost its rich, olive tone.

How the hell did I wake them up? Was the fucking portal booby trapped? Was that even possible?

I needed Jerry, but first I'd check on whether the necromancer coven was still hanging around.

Lost in my own thoughts, I crashed into Dacey coming around the corner.

"Shit," I hissed, reaching out to steady her. "Are you okay?"

She nodded, a nervous smile pulling at her lips. "We never get to do anything fun," she confided.

"This is fun?" I asked.

She nodded enthusiastically. "Mermaids and unicorns. Awesome."

"Dacey, did everyone stay?"

"No, just me and Jaelle."

I nodded. "Where is she?"

"Sleeping. She'd never let me explore on my own. Says I'm too important to be in danger."

I nodded, "Our house is safe."

"That's what I told her!"

I smiled at her childlike glee.

"Can you take a look at Amin for me? I'm hitting a dead end trying to wake them up."

"I should get Jaelle," Dacey said, suddenly nervous.

"Sure, go ahead."

She nodded, heading back down the hallway.

Anna came up behind me. "We need Jerry."

"Agreed, I'm going to get my phone from the bedroom. I want Jaelle and Dacey to look in on Amin. Something isn't right."

"You mean the fact that they haven't woken up?" Anna asked me in a huff.

I growled at her. "I mean I think they're dying."

With that truth bomb, I walked away to my room.

Logan was still sleeping, as was Ginny.

I felt badly about calling Jerry, especially when he had a new baby to tend to, but I needed help.

He picked up on the third ring. "What's wrong?" he rasped into the phone.

"Can a portal be booby trapped?" I asked without preamble.

Jerry groaned, "Yes, but it would take—"

"A Fae?" I asked, finishing his sentence.

Jerry sighed, "Yes, exceptional power."

"I think they're dying," I confessed, slowing my gait down the stairs.

"What do you need from me?" I was grateful for his commitment to me.

"The books I brought back, can you look at them? Anna and I can't make heads or tails. I'm going to have the necromancers look at Amin, see if there's anything they can do."

"Their specialty is death," Jerry reminded me.

"And mine is killing, but that doesn't stop me from saving innocent lives."

"Alright, I'll be right over. Can we bring Greta?" Jerry asked.

"We haven't decided that is her name," Mark said from the background.

I laughed, "Yeah, I think we still have Ginny's pack-and-play. And I agree with Mark, not Greta."

Jerry huffed, "It's a form of Gretchen."

My heart constricted painfully. Gretchen was Grams's given name. I hadn't thought of her much with everything going on, but I missed her still.

I cleared my throat. "Grams would agree, the kid needs a better name."

Jerry sighed. "Well, we can't keep calling her sweet pea."

I laughed. "Take your time, she won't know the difference."

"I suppose," he grumbled. "See you soon."

I hung up, coming to join Dacey and Jaelle outside of Amin's door.

"This does not bode well," Jaelle stated.

"Nothing ever fucking does," I mumbled. Anna gave me a pointed glare and I cleared my throat. "What exactly doesn't bode well?" I asked.

"Death energy, it's slipping out under the door, coating it, overlapping itself. It's not natural, death energy doesn't usually behave in this manner," Dacey explained, her eyes roving over things I couldn't see.

I opened the door to Amin's room and they both stepped back.

"Close the door!" hissed Jaelle.

I did as she requested. "What's wrong?"

"I don't think it's sentient," Dacey whispered.

Jaelle shook her head. "Why would you bring us into such a dangerous situation? We have done nothing to you," she snapped at me.

I narrowed my eyes at her. "Because we needed help. Because I saved your ass, because you owe me. You can bury your head in the sand another day. Today, I need you to help me wake up Amin and my father."

"Why? Why do these two matter so much?"

"They are my charges, my responsibilities. I will not fail them."

"For what purpose?" she hissed at me.

"The Fae are on Earth, along with the Succubus Queen. We need everyone and every advantage to fight them off," Anna said, keeping her composure far better than myself.

Jaelle shook her head, clenching her jaw. "Why should we believe you?"

"Aside from the fact you saw us get spewed from a portal?" Anna asked.

I silently raised my eyebrow at Jaelle.

She tried another line of reasoning. "We don't follow under leadership."

"You are testing my limited patience, Jaelle," I groaned. "Why does this have to be so damn difficult?"

Wariness passed behind her gaze before it hardened, her arm instinctually wrapping around the younger Dacey.

I groaned and Anna asked, "What do you know that you aren't telling us?"

Dacey sighed, "Can we sit somewhere?"

I nodded, heading back to the kitchen. Dacey and Jaelle sat on one side of the farm table and Anna on the other. I filled four coffee cups, restarting the pot for when Logan got up.

I set the cups on the table, going back to the fridge for creamer and fetching the sugar, setting everything between us on the table as I sat down next to Anna.

Drumming my fingers, I watched Dacey spoon the sugar in, followed by creamer. She took a long swig, meeting my glare for a moment before she cleared her throat and set the cup down.

"There is a prophecy," she began. I swallowed my groan, Anna didn't.

"See, I told you they wouldn't respect our traditions," hissed Jaelle.

Dacey gave Jaelle an annoyed look.

I in turn shot a pointed look toward Anna. "Please continue," I encouraged.

Dacey returned her attention to me. I studied her gray eyes, flecked with baby blue. Her skin was still perfection, unblemished by wrinkles or time.

She twirled a golden lock around her finger. "The prophecy in its simplest form claims that the Fae will retake Earth as their playground. That humans will face extinction and the Supernaturals as a whole will have to rise up and send the Fae back to their world."

Anna huffed, "That's fucking accurate."

I swallowed. "Too accurate."

Dacey nodded. "In dealing with death, we often find ourselves the keepers of possible futures."

I didn't know what to say to that.

"A little warning would have been nice," Anna grumbled.

"Possible futures," I repeated. "You have multiple prophecies?" I asked.

Dacey nodded. "It's my job to record them." She tucked a strand of hair behind her ear, looking down at her hands. "Something about this one was different. The way the details were given, the description of events..." Her voice trailed off.

"It led us to cut ties with the rest of the Supernatural word," Jaelle supplied, filling in Dacey's silence.

I turned my attention to her. "Why?"

"Because one of the possible outcomes is the enslavement and destruction," she hissed at me, "of all Supernaturals."

Anna shook her head. "So you thought ... what? Avoiding the problem would make it go away?"

"Possible futures," Jaelle hissed at Anna. "I was hoping it wouldn't come to this."

I sighed. "Is there anything else in the prophecies that can help us?" I asked.

Dacey shook her head. "Much has come to pass, much is still in limbo." It was like talking to the damn Oracle.

"Don't ask what the future will be," Jaelle warned.

"The future is what we make it," Anna responded.

I nodded. "We've dealt with the uncertainty of prophecies before. What is going to happen cannot be stopped. All we can do is make the best decisions for our dependents."

The door to the garage opened and sleepy but content Jerry and Mark ambled in.

"Oh sweet, beautiful coffee, come to daddy," Jerry whispered.

Mark laughed loudly, hauling in a car seat. Jerry looked at him, confused for a moment before realizing what he had just said, then smiling widely at his mate. I couldn't help but grin myself as I watched their interactions.

Mark set the baby down on the table in her car seat, rubbing his eyes. "She finally fell asleep."

I chuckled. "The portal must have been draining on her, not to mention almost being starved."

"We took her into urgent care, and she came out with a clean bill of heath. ...Tommy got us the documentation," Jerry admitted after a moment's hesitation.

I grunted, "That kid learns new tricks every day."

I felt Logan awaken.

Downstairs, dealing with shit.

He growled, even in my head, displeasure at not being included and waking up without me ringing clear through the bond.

I pushed his annoyance away. I had plenty of my own.

"Jerry, I need you to work with Jaelle and Dacey to get everything they need to kill whatever is keeping Amin and my father asleep."

He nodded, taking a sip of his coffee as I stood. "What are you going to do?" Anna asked me.

"That depends, do you want to take the unicorns to their new home, go property shopping with the mermaids, or work with Tommy on tracking down leads for possible hideouts of our mother?"

Anna's face wrinkled in disdain. Logan entered the kitchen. "Let Hudson take the unicorns to their home. He can shift and lead them there. We plotted out a course last night. I'll send a car along as back up."

I nodded. "Mermaids?" I asked Anna.

She huffed, standing with a grunt. "Mermaids," she agreed.

I chuckled, going to kiss Logan good morning. "It's too damn early," he complained.

"I know. I couldn't sleep."

He grunted, going for the coffee. I headed to Tommy's room, pausing outside his door, deciding to call Becky instead.

She answered groggily, "What's up, boss?" I hated when she called me that.

"I need you to look into the incident that happened with the giant Fae tree, see if you can pinpoint any anomalies and if any other locations in the country have them."

Becky grunted, "Even in Garrick's territory?"

"Yes, everywhere. I think something else came through that night."

"The Tree was a distraction?"

"Possibly, or an unforeseen consequence."

"On it," Becky ended the call. At least she didn't call me boss again.

I pondered for a moment outside of Tommy's room. Did I wake him up and get him on the case, too? Or just let Tommy rest and trust Becky on this one? I sighed. I needed to try and let Tommy be a kid. He had already proven to be an asset and I'd have plenty of additional opportunities to test his skills.

I was headed back to the kitchen when the doorbell sounded. I felt Logan's concern and worry blast through the mate mark. No one should have gotten past the guard gate. I was running to the front door.

"Stay in your rooms!" I yelled as doors began to crack open. I stormed down the stairs, sliding to a stop next to a hideous end table, gaudy as hell. I assumed Lorraine had picked it out. The twisted design hid a gun safe operated by a fingerprint scanner, bolted through the wood and into the concrete. That was the only reason it was still here.

Dammit, I could use Anna, and Hudson.

Logan stood poised at the door, waiting, his eyes darkening when they landed on me. The pit of dread grew in my stomach. Casting a quick glance at the kitchen, I saw Jerry, Jaelle and Dacey standing back a few paces. All eyes were riveted to the monitor by the door. I was glad Mark and the baby were out of sight.

I looked up to see a familiar face and small-statured body, fear churning in my gut.

I depressed the talk button on the monitor. "What are you doing here, Bob?"

"Four—or, excuse me, Olivia. I have come to negotiate the terms of your assistance," Bob merrily replied, as though a Fae showing up on my doorstep wasn't the worst of nightmares.

"Assistance for what?" I demanded.

Bob fidgeted, steepling his fingers in front of him and drumming them together one by one. "I'd appreciate an audience with you, face to face."

I grunted, "Fine, but not here."

Bob nodded, "You don't trust me."

He almost sounded sad about that fact.

"Nothing personal, Bob. The Fae and I don't have the best track record together."

He nodded again. "I understand. In the park then, next to the coffee house?"

"Yeah, just give me a few minutes to get dressed."

Bob smiled and disappeared.

"Fucking creepy," Jerry whispered, shaking.

I wanted to put all the children into the panic room and demand they never leave. This was a threat I was woefully unprepared to destroy.

I turned to Jerry and the necromancers. "Get working on the list. I need my father awake if any of us plan to survive the Fae." My words were a harsh whisper; I didn't believe for a second Bob was really gone.

As one, they nodded shakily. Logan and I were hot up the stairs and into our room.

"You are scared," he said as I pulled on my leather pants.

"Scared doesn't begin to cover how fucking terrified I am. I don't know how to kill the Fae, fuck I can't even injure one unless I for some reason find myself with Anna and a magic sword. That damn tree was probably a distraction so whatever the fuck else came through could."

"You've never failed the children, Olie." He wasn't moving fast enough for me.

"We've never gone up against the Fae, Logan." I strapped my double swords on, feeling better the second their comfortable weight settled onto my shoulders.

He nodded, looking over my leather jacket, sword, dagger, and guns. At least I was leaving the crossbow here. I still hadn't called Myrtle for that damn flamethrower.

"I need a flamethrower."

Logan raised his eyebrow at me, clearly not understanding my sheer panic. I hope he never did.

"Let's go," I said, rushing past him.

...

The walk to the park was painfully long. Was he hurting someone? Did some kid walk too close to him? Was he planning on an epic display of power? What sick shit was I going to find? I thought about taking the SUV, but I needed to move. To try to gather my thoughts, to form several plans.

How the fuck had Bob found me? Could my mother find me as easily? What about Luharposn? That thought chilled my insides and was the only thing I could focus on. I'd give myself up now if it saved Logan and the children the horror of that soulless creature.

Bob was waiting at a picnic table, a coffee perched in front of him and a peaceful smile on his worn, brown face.

I never altered my gait as I approached, taking the seat across from him and resting my arms on the table.

"How did you find me?" Right to the point.

"A homing spell from the blood you left in the world I believe you refer to as Red."

"Can anyone do that?" I asked.

"Only the most skilled Fae can track across dimensions." My gut said he was telling the truth. My head warred with me on it.

I wanted to ask if Luharposn was a skilled Fae, but that felt too much like tipping my hand.

"I'm afraid he is."

"Dammit," I hissed.

"You can read minds?" Logan asked, sitting down next to me.

Bob shrugged. "Not all minds, but Olivia's is unusually open. Aside from that, I know her fear of Luharposn. I have watched her a long time and understand her need to protect her charges."

I didn't know what to make of that. Except that it unnerved me to no end, so much so that I tore my mind from thinking about it.

"What did you want to discuss?" I asked.

Bob sighed, his frail arms coming to rest on the table as he looked down into his coffee. "It is with a grave heart that I regret to inform you the Queen has been taken."

My brows drew down. "My mother?" I asked, confused.

Bob shook his head, waving a dismissive hand. "No, The Queen of the Fae. Your mother volunteered to help Luharposn's insanity."

"Not surprised there. What happened to everyone in that world?" I asked.

"Most would be dead. Luharposn would need to consume their energy to fuel his magic in order to steal our Queen and transport to Earth."

"Why Earth?" Logan asked.

"He has grown bored on Fae. The Queen wouldn't allow him to use Earth as an entertainment source, though."

"So, he took her to amuse himself?" I asked.

"Yes."

"That's insane," Logan grumbled. Yeah, I couldn't disagree there. Boredom had Luharposn kidnapping the Fae Queen, freeing my mother, and killing my people. I fucking hated that man.

"I'm afraid Luharposn's advanced age has caused his mental faculties not to function as well as they once did," Bob explained.

"What do you want from us?" I asked.

"Your help in getting The Queen back."

"What do we get in return?" I asked.

"What do you want?"

"Cure The Magician and Amin—"

"Done," Bob said quickly.

"Assist if needed in breaking through the blocks of my magic—"

Bob waved a hand, yawning, "Easily."

"Tell me how to kill Luharposn."

"No." The answer was instant. "I can do many things, but not that."

"Fine, then I reserve a final favor."

Bob nodded, "Agreed." I really should be asking for more, I realized. He was quick to give me almost anything I wanted.

"What of The Succubus Queen?" Logan asked.

"What happens to her is of no consequence." Bob dismissed it with a wave of his hand.

"Luharposn?" I asked.

Bob's large brown eyes rested on me. "The Queen will want him, if he's alive when we free her."

"I guess killing him will be my first priority, then."

Bob nodded seriously. "So long as you get the Queen back unharmed."

"We can't guarantee unharmed," Logan added.

Bob shifted in his seat. "Smart lion," he conceded.

"I accept your terms," he agreed after a moment.

He held out his hand and I looked at it warily.

"I don't suppose I have much of a choice," I whispered.

"No, not unless you want the necromancers, mage, Magician and djinn to die."

I blew out a breath as he casually listed off the death toll. Gritting my jaw, I held out my hand. "We have an agreement."

"Lovely, now let's go cure your father."

...

I was leery about letting Bob into the house, but also helpless.

"Do not hurt my charges," I warned him softly.

"I do not harm children," he answered, annoyed.

I grunted, opening the door and following him in.

He paused and moved to the side, crossing his arms and tapping his foot. I narrowed my eyes at him, wondering what was making him nervous.

"This way," I muttered, moving to Amin's room first. I opened the door and headed inside, Bob following me.

"You don't like our home," Logan commented, closing the door behind us.

Bob cast Logan a look before going to sit next to Amin. "I have no issue with your home, but your father..." Bob looked over at me and I raised my head, intrigued. "We didn't leave things very well between us."

"You are the reason the unicorns called him a liar." I was making a statement and regretting trusting a Fae.

"I am." Bob didn't elaborate, and I was more concerned about his ability to wake Amin up without killing him.

"I wonder, however did you come to obtain a djinn," Bob stated or maybe asked, but I wasn't telling him. He knew too fucking much about me already.

Bob sighed, touching Amin's forehead. A brilliant orb manifested there, absorbing into Amin's skin before disappearing. Amin's eyes snapped open with a powerful inhale.

"Welcome back," Bob said, standing up and stepping back. Amin sat up, swinging his long legs over the bed.

"What happened?" he asked, holding his head in his hands.

"The portal was booby trapped," I told him.

Amin shook his head, looking at Bob. "Fae?" he asked.

Bob nodded.

"You don't like the Fae," Amin stated, looking at me.

I grunted, how the fuck did he know that?

"Desperate times, now let's wake my father up."

Bob sighed, following me out as Logan brought up the rear. I knocked gently on the door to my father's room, waiting for Doyle. His movements were slower, his clothing hanging loose.

Doyle snorted, looking behind me at Bob.

"No!" he rumbled, trying to close the door.

"Dammit," I hissed, stopping the door with my foot. "He woke Amin up."

Doyle paused in crushing my foot. "He can't be trusted. You know this!"

I sighed, why was everyone telling me what I already knew?

"I don't trust him, but we need his help and he needs us. The arrangement is temporary."

Doyle rumbled, "If he harms The Magician—"

I rested a hand on Doyle's arm, pushing the door open. "I know, Doyle, I know."

Doyle finally relented, nodding as he opened the door fully. I blew out a breath, going to stand by my father's head.

Bob sat down on the bed, watching me, his light form hardly denting the mattress. "You care for him."

I thought about telling him about the memory Baqer had given me, but shrugged instead. "He is family," I finally answered. And whatever complicate mess that entailed.

Bob didn't miss my pause. "Indeed."

He repeated the touch to the forehead with a brilliant orb. My father's eyes opened; a breath later, he grabbed Bob's thin wrist.

I saw Bob swallow. "Magician," he greeted my father.

"Bob," my father wheezed. His gaze swung up to me. "Daughter," he whispered, releasing Bob, who moved away from him quickly.

"Easy," I counseled, moving to steady him in his attempt to stand. "The portal was booby trapped."

"How did you return? Amin?" he asked, working on putting the pieces of his missing days together.

I shook my head. "We blended two spells and blood to open a portal from there."

He nodded, rubbing his forehead and lying back down. "I should have known you would have found a way." His gaze swung to Bob. "What is he doing here?"

I sighed. "We needed his help to wake you and Amin up. He needs our help to free The Fae Queen from Luharposn."

The Magician's gaze cut to Bob.

"She did a fine job of negotiating," Bob offered. "Even demanded I help, if needed, freeing her power."

The Magician grunted, pushing slowly into a sitting position. I moved to help him up.

"Not to mention a favor yet to come," Logan added, leaning against the doorway.

That caught my dad's attention. He gave me a slow, approving nod. A loud snore had me turning to see Doyle, passed out.

I huffed, pulling out a spare blanket from the closet and draping it over him.

"He watched over you," I said to no one in particular. My father might have claimed Doyle was my guardian, but I didn't think so.

I turned, debating my next move. Finding where my mother and the monster Fae were hiding out was going to do me no good if I couldn't kill them both.

What about those untapped powers Anna displayed in the red world library?

"Where is Anna?" I asked Logan. His superb hearing didn't leave room for many secrets in our house. He tilted his head, listening.

"With Ginny," he rumbled.

I nodded. "Who is Anna?" Bob asked, very interested in my business.

I turned, debating, searching his earnest face that begged to be trusted. "Anna was Seven."

Understanding dawned in his overly large brown eyes. "Seven," he repeated thoughtfully.

I nodded. Bob raised his chin, eyeing me warily.

I rolled my eyes, answering his unasked question. "Yes, I know who her father is, and so does she."

His brow furrowed. "Who told you?"

It was my turn to furrow my brow. "Explain why it matters."

"She was not supposed to know," he hissed at me, no longer the benign helper.

"Too late," I snipped back. "Does she have hidden power as well?" I demanded.

His lips thinned into an invisible line. That answered that question.

"Do not use your favor, let us see if we can unlock her power first," my father counseled.

I nodded.

"You probably need to rest—" I began.

My father waved me off. "No, I'm done resting." He looked at Doyle. "Food would be good, though."

I nodded, heading outside the room, finding Amin waiting for us.

He nodded, cautiously looking at Bob. "Can I speak with you?" he asked me.

I led him down the hallway, uneasy about leaving Bob, but trusting Logan could handle it.

I ushered him into Ali and Grant's office, currently unoccupied. I closed the door, waiting for him to speak.

He fidgeted silently.

"What?" I asked.

"You saved my life," was his response.

"Yep." Pretty sure this conversation didn't need a closed door.

Amin crossed his arms over his chest. "You do not use me. You just saved me. Do you not know how this relationship is supposed to work?"

"Amin, you are a person. I don't want to use you. I will, as recently evidenced, need your help, but I'd like to think it's because we are friends, not because I'm your master." I hated saying that word.

His dark eyes regarded me silently for long moments.

"I'm not known for my patience, Amin."

"It's a dangerous path you walk," he warned gravely.

"Not new information," I groaned. "I'm currently working with a Fae, trying to unlock some hidden power in myself and Anna, all the while hoping that our powers will allow us to kill an exceptionally powerful Fae and my mother."

Amin shook his head. I wasn't understanding what he was trying to convey.

"If you don't need me, I have affairs to attend to," he finally supplied.

I nodded. "I appreciate the help."

With that he was gone. I stared at the space he had occupied for a long moment. I didn't understand the djinn at all. How was a being that powerful trapped into serving me? Or really, serving at all?

I groaned, whatever. I had enough shit to worry about without adding how and why the djinn got where they were.

Where are you? I sent to Logan.

Kitchen, he answered. My favorite spot.

I did a double take at Bob sitting at the farm style table, swinging his short legs. His dirty rags hung loose around his body, which made no sense for a being with more power in his pinky finger than I had ever seen.

Again, not my issue. He wasn't a friend, he wasn't an ally, he was a means to an end and I never, ever wanted to see him again after I finished this job.

I should use my favor to learn how to ward against the Fae, I mused.

"You didn't tell me you killed Baqer," Bob said, not turning at my entrance.

I shot Anna a warning glare. "Well, we did."

"How interesting," he muttered.

I was tempted to ask why that was interesting, but I refrained. I wasn't giving Bob any additional information, nor was I tipping my hand on just how dumb I was in relation to the Fae.

I sighed. It was going to be a trial-and-error process regarding how to kill the fuckers, which didn't appeal to me at all.

Bob tilted his head, and I paid close attention to the movement, watching his eye staring unfocused at a random spot of floor tile.

"I am needed elsewhere," Bob relayed.

I nodded, my gaze cutting to my father.

"We will begin preparations for unlocking their power." My father's gaze pinned Bob, who shifted in his seat.

"I suppose you will be needing this," Bob muttered before winking out.

My head snapped around, checking the room for him, not believing for a second he had actually left.

My father sighed, sitting down heavily in front of me, picking up the small brown pouch tied with twine and pocketing it.

"He is gone, daughter," my father reassured, turning his attention to his breakfast, shoveling a bite.

"How can you be so certain?" I questioned him, narrowing my eyes.

"Only a few, rare Fae can speak without words. Whoever called him, he listened."

I grunted, slouching down, drumming my fingers against the wood table.

"We need a dragon," Doyle grunted. I turned to see him eating, standing at the breakfast bar. We needed a bigger table for him.

Anna laughed, "A dragon?"

I chewed on my thumbnail, turning to my father.

He cleared his throat, dabbing his mouth with a napkin. "Yes," he confirmed, his gaze piercing mine. "Dragons were rare when we belonged to this world before, but they could be found."

I grunted. "Pure-blooded dragon?"

My father nodded.

I looked to Logan. "I need to call Garrick."

Chapter 8

Garrick had demanded to meet me in person for my request.

Logan put my SUV into park in front of the hotel and spa in Aspen Colorado.

"You actually stayed here?" he asked as we exited the vehicle.

I looked over the perfectly sculpted marble fountain and spiral-trimmed trees. Definitely not my usual choice in accommodations.

I shrugged, meeting him at the back. "It was within walking distance of one of the hot spots I was investigating."

"When were you here, again?" Logan asked.

"When Ginny was born," I answered, looking over at him.

Logan paused in gathering our bags.

"This was the sex ring?" he asked.

"Yeah, one of the women the assholes took is a quarter dragon, her father is half dragon. I'm hoping grandma or grandpa is still around."

My father and Doyle got out of the backseat, Doyle properly disguised, the news conference announcing his presence delayed. I didn't relish the idea of drawing undue attention to us. So much so, I had forgone my dual swords.

I had decided to leave Anna at home. This process was unknown and undoubtedly dangerous. I didn't need both of us kicking the bucket in an attempt to unlock our power. If this worked, I'd bring her back with me ... if we found the dragon ... if my father told me what Bob had left ... if we defeated the Fae.

I just didn't trust anyone. My gaze shifted to the lion shifter at my side. Actually, I suppose that wasn't true anymore, or it shouldn't have been. I trusted Logan, I think I did.

I didn't want to dwell on it. I'd just end up feeling guiltier, if that was possible, for him being stuck with me.

The glass doors to the hotel and spa opened. I looked around the deserted lobby for Garrick.

Logan branched off, heading toward the young woman behind the counter, who greeted him with an overly friendly smile. I watched her eyes slide over his bulging biceps and chest as he easily carried our bags.

My feet were moving before I could register the blinding jealously shooting through my body.

"Olivia." A hand on my forearm had me turning to the rich timbre of Garrick. I raised an eyebrow at him.

"Where have you been lurking?" I questioned him.

He smirked at my ire, linking our arms together. "Come now, dear girl, lurking is such a distasteful word."

"But accurate." Garrick tried to pull me along away from Logan, but I wasn't moving until Logan was done checking us in.

"Jealous much, love?" Garrick asked.

I huffed a noncommittal response, staring daggers. The hotel clerk gave a playful laugh. My eyes narrowed and Garrick laughed at my side.

Feeling my jealousy, Logan turned, raising a questioning eyebrow.

I huffed, turning to Garrick, who was staring behind me. "You didn't mention you had guests."

I glanced back at my father and Doyle before returning my attention to Garrick with a shrug. "We have guests." I didn't mean for it to sound like either a question or an apology.

Garrick moved to Doyle with that damn vamp speed. "I don't believe we've been properly introduced. I'm Garrick, Olivia's counterpart on the Supernatural Council of the West."

"Doyle," the minotaur rumbled. Garrick nodded before casting me a suspicious and annoyed glance.

I crossed my arms over my chest, glaring back at him. My father broke our staring contest, coming to stand between us, his back blocking out Garrick. "I am The Magician, Olivia's father."

Garrick jerked, peering around my father. "Father?" he asked me incredulously.

I nodded and shrugged.

Garrick shook hands with him, his clever mind working overtime. He adjusted his shirt sleeves down under his jacket in a rare moment of uncertainty.

"Why Olivia, aren't you just full of surprises?" Garrick asked me in amused wonder.

I continued to scowl as Logan finished with the flirt and took my hand. He found my jealously amusing. Asshole.

Garrick turned his attention back to my father. "It's a pleasure to meet you. And here we had thought Olivia was created in a lab."

At least that explanation had made sense and didn't leave me wondering why my father had abandoned me. Logan squeezed my hand.

"Your name is Magician?" Garrick asked, turning so my father's back wasn't to me.

"Not originally," my father answered, "but it is what I am called now."

Garrick nodded, seeming to understand. I suppose when you've lived as many lifetimes as he had, reinventing yourself was necessary.

I wondered briefly what my father's name might have been before, but decided I didn't care. A name didn't change who he was and what he had done.

Garrick escorted us to the rooms, leaving Doyle and the Magician at theirs and dropping down into a navy sofa in ours. The room looked out onto the wilderness.

"I took the liberty of renting the rest of the rooms out," he admitted, unbuttoning his jacket, leaning an arm over the armrest.

"Why?" I asked, spreading my weapons collection over the small kitchen table.

He shrugged before meeting my gaze. "Tell me this isn't Fae related."

I groaned, dropping into a chair to face him. "I suppose I owe you an explanation."

I felt Logan's shock through the bond. It was warranted—anyone else I would have told to fuck off and mind their own business. But Garrick and I fought for the same things—more importantly, against the same things.

"We've had a few issues," I admitted.

"The giant tree?"

"Yes, the giant tree was the start. Anna and I went back to our home world and encountered another Fae we killed, but not before he told us our mother had joined with the Fae. I believe the tree was either a distraction or an unforeseen consequence of them coming to Earth."

Garrick looked at me, dumbfounded.

"Right, so I also have a mother, who is the Queen of the succubi and a roaring bitch. Anna is my half-sister, same mother."

He just kept blinking at me.

"How was she able to contact the Fae?" he finally asked, that wicked smart brain piecing together my current dilemma.

I shook my head. "I don't know, but given that Anna's father is Luharposn, she probably had a way."

"Anna's half Fae?!" Garrick sat back, quickly absorbing that information, his gaze out of focus for a brief moment before it snapped back to me. "And you're half magician."

I nodded. "Anna's powers and mine are bound, which is why they only lend themselves to us in life or death situations."

Logan answered the knock on the door, admitting my father and Doyle.

"What are you hoping to achieve here in my territory?" Garrick asked. I didn't need the reminder we were on his turf.

"A dragon. When I was here last, I encountered a half-dragon being and his quarter-dragon daughter. I'm hoping I can track them down again and find the full-blooded kind." I gave thought to reminding him that I was the only reason his executioners had been released unharmed, but I'd be irritated at such a reminder myself. Plus, he wasn't actually fighting me on anything, just bitching.

Garrick nodded, his eyes solemn. "Nothing good can come of the Fae being here."

I sighed, "I know. I suppose this isn't the best time to admit I agreed to work with Bob."

Garrick slammed his hand down on the armrest, his eyes darkening in rage, fangs peeking out. Oh fuck, he was pissed.

As quickly as the white incisors appeared, they vanished. "I'd inform you how foolish that decision is, but—"

"But I already know," I agreed. "Luharposn took the Fae Queen. He's acting rogue. At least that is what Bob tells me."

Garrick sighed, rubbing his forehead. "I highly doubt you have the entire story."

I said nothing; I had already thought the same thing.

Finally, I offered, "That doesn't change the end goal: kill the Fae or drive them out."

Nothing good could come of the Fae, duh.

Chapter 9

Unlike Logan and Garrick, I was dressed for the frigid weather. My father had adapted to his updated clothing as well. Doyle was cloaked, and looking mighty disagreeable about the whole situation.

I should have cared, but I had bigger issues than his dislike of being dishonest.

I exhaled a breath at the mouth of the cave, running a hand over the rough stone. "Nila?" I called out. If this was their home, then knocking is the polite thing to do, right?

"Are you going in there?" Garrick asked with a laugh, standing behind me on the railroad tracks.

I grunted affirmative, moving forward.

"Nila?" I tried again. I didn't really expect her to be there. While her dad had been holed up in the cave with two of Garrick's executioners, I couldn't see this being an ideal spot to call home. But I had zero other leads on where to find a basically extinct species. Nila hadn't left me a forwarding address.

"Nila, it's Olivia." Hopefully, she remembered me. I felt like being kidnapped by a human sex ring and then the two of us killing together should have left a lasting impression.

It should, Logan agreed.

I huffed, casting him a look, not realizing I was broadcasting my thoughts. He shrugged with a smile. He had easily adjusted to being in my head and accessing not only my emotional state, which any sexual partner of mine would have access to, but also very specific thoughts.

When we'd first had mated, I could easily read the thoughts of all the individual pack members, but since getting shot and visiting the red world of doom as a spirit being, I didn't have the same potency. On one hand, I appreciated it—having to block all of those voices had been intense. But having the ability to hear them had also helped me save Logan.

I sighed, linking my hand with his roughly calloused one. The movement caused him to pause, examining me.

"What?" I asked, clicking on my flashlight.

"We will wait for you here!" Garrick yelled after us. I swear that damn man was laughing at me, the whole thing was such a long shot.

I huffed an answer under my breath, knowing full well that with his superior vampire hearing, it would be heard.

I swept the vast cavern, which reminded me of the inside of a bread bowl, turned upside down.

Abandoned rail cars had been tossed about, pick axes were rusting over, and broken track littered the floor along with caving-in plastic hard hats.

"There are two tunnels in the back," Logan informed me, pulling me in that direction.

"You know which one to take." It wasn't a question.

"There is something down here," he agreed.

"Any ideas on what?" Asking "who" seemed pointless, as he had said something.

I cast a glance at him, the flashlight's glow not dissipating the darkness much as he tilted his head. He really was handsome, deliciously so. Strong brows, gorgeously chiseled cheekbones, and a sinfully talented mouth.

"Stop it," he grunted, giving my hand a squeeze.

I smiled at him, my absolute worry about the Fae, tempered by hope. Even though we had lost Grams, and it hurt, deeply and wholly, I had him. This alliance, this powerful love that I never dreamed possible.

He stopped walking, following my thoughts and emotions with his own.

"You are mine, Olivia, from now until the end of time." His voice was soft, full of the unspoken need, desire that went far beyond sexual appetite. Our souls had become intertwined, and I ... I was becoming a damn softie.

"I need to kill something," I huffed, looking past Logan, who laughed.

"Holy fuck," I whispered. I pulled Logan toward me, stepping back. Not one to be led anywhere, he turned. We both looked into one purple, cat-slanted iris, taller than our combined heights.

"Nila?" I tried, my voice a squeak.

It blinked. Where the fuck was the other eye?

With a huff of smoke, the dragon lifted its head, towering over us, and conveniently answering my unspoken question. Apparently, we'd had a side view, and I was now questioning just how its eyes turned if that was a side view.

The dragon lumbered up, and the damn cave shook.

"So, thoughts on running outside?" I asked.

A large, purple-scaled tail slammed next to us.

"Olie, are you scared?" Logan teased. Seriously, in a time like this, the asshole was teasing.

"No." I was lying. There was a giant, winged, well I think winged, DRAGON heading toward us. Yeah, I was a little freaked out.

"We require your assistance," Logan said to the dragon. Well, at least one of us was keeping the goal in mind. Right, and what exactly did I need from said dragon? Things I should have asked my father about previously...

The dragon growled and it wasn't the usual shifter growl I was used to ignoring. The timbre was all wrong, deeper, with an extra nasty snarl just for fun.

"No need to be an asshole," I whispered. Whatever, I wasn't scared. The dragon slammed its clawed foot down, shaking loose rocks and debris from above us.

Great idea, call the hulking reptile an asshole, Logan scolded.

Fire spewed at us next. We split up, dodging the blast. My flashlight was smashed, thrown from my hand, and I cursed again. Now I was blind, well except for the reflective dragon eyes following me.

"Do you think it's playing dumb?" I yelled at Logan, pulling a sword once I regained my footing.

"I don't think it's playing at anything," he responded calmly.

Yeah, I got that. Couldn't disagree with that logic.

Heavy, lumbering footsteps rocked the ground under our feet, making obtaining a fighting stance difficult. Not that an effective fighting stance was going to make a difference against a massive, hulking, fire-breathing DRAGON!

"I take it you found the dragon?" Garrick called in, amusement coloring his voice.

I looked toward the entrance in annoyance.

"Nope, sure didn't!" I yelled.

Let's take this fight outside, I can't see what the hell I'm doing and I sure as fuck don't know what I actually need to do with said found dragon, I told Logan.

I felt Logan's agreement, he was not one to enjoy being caught off guard and without a plan. Neither of us had expected to find the dragon this easily. Perhaps fate was smiling on us, maybe this was our break to keep our small world safe. Or maybe we were both about to be incinerated. Fifty-fifty.

Logan unflinchingly stayed on my right side, between me and danger, even with the thundering and earth-shaking noises there.

The dragon gave a roar of clear irritation. We exploded out of the cavern, the scaly overgrown lizard still after us and fire nipping at our heels.

"Tell me what I'm after here!" I yelled toward my father, the small band of ancient and powerful beings staying clear of the entrance. The Magician stared behind me in awe, his mouth hanging open. Not helpful.

"Ride and name the beast!" he screamed at me, recovering from his earlier stupor. He scrambled back farther, Doyle bracing him against falling, no doubt feeling the heat of the dragon's fire.

I felt Logan shift, pulling energy from the packs to make the transition seamless between one step and the next. That was a neat trick. A towering, caramel-colored lion padded at my side, far faster than my own two feet.

"Logan, go left!" I screamed in our mad dash.

NO! I'm not leaving you here to die a fiery death.

"Trust me!" I shoved him left before darting to the right. Not that one really shoves a furry cat weighing hundreds of pounds. The mate bond kicked into overdrive as he monitored me.

What hell is wrong with you?

It's a daunting list, how much time do you have?

He growled. I couldn't help the laugh bubbling up, this was it! I was going to get my magic and we were going to kick some Fae ass!

The ground dipped down, my speed making the descent dangerous. Well, not as dangerous as the giant lizard trying to chomp my ass. I dodged low-slung branches and fallen logs, all while trying to stay ahead of the ten-thousand-pound, allegedly mythical beast pounding after me.

I ran hard over the pine-needled ground, hoping and searching for what I thought I remembered from my last trip there. In my study of the terrain, I had found a deep ravine where I, personally, would have thrown the bodies of all those I was trying to get rid of. It was on my list to check for Garrick's missing executioners. However, I'd found them before wasting time perusing the gorge.

Be fucking careful. I am not losing you. In fact, I will kill your father. I was pretty sure Logan could follow my train of thought on where this was going.

Such a worrier, I chided him, pushing down my own concern. Where the fuck was it? The damn fairytale beast was snapping at my heels. I took my eyes off the clear ground in front of me for a moment to look around in case I was missing what I wanted.

My foot came down wrong and I pitched forward, rolling, the downward slope rapidly accelerating my pace.

But good news! I had found the damn gorge. My stomach pitched as gravity pulled me down and off the edge. I swallowed a scream, twisting around, scrambling for purchase. This wasn't exactly my poorly thought out plan, but hopefully the results would be the same.

I felt Logan's screaming, but was a little distracted.

...

Logan's heart stopped beating, he was certain of it. Cold fear drained both his strength and the warmth from his shifter hide as he watched Olivia pitch over the edge. He had been easily loping behind them, watching to see what insane, poorly put together, half-formed idea Olivia had dreamed up. He typically enjoyed her spontaneity, but not when it put her damn life on the line.

From the brief glimpses, even she must have thought it was reckless, but falling off a damn cliff, that couldn't have been part of her plan. Right?

Yet it almost seemed like the dragon was holding back, which gave him pause to retain rational thought.

He searched the mate bond. Finding Olivia alive, he held onto her through the bond, as though that alone would keep her alive.

He heard her laugher, bubbling and rich. Relief washed though his limbs, making him weak as he padded to the edge of the ravine.

The air whooshed by him as Olie rode upside down on the dragon's neck, yelling at it.

....

Logan's bewildered lion face was priceless as I soared overhead, attached to the wrong side of a dragon's neck.

My plan is working! I told Logan excitedly.

Your plan is insane, he noted.

I had been fairly certain that once I had attached myself to the scaly reptile, it wouldn't be willing to die just to spite me.

My gamble had paid off, a whoosh of air being displaced as the large beast pumped its wings. Okay, so now I only had to hold on until we were on solid ground again. I opened my eyes and the ground spun away from us. Shit, not part of my plan.

I closed my eyes again as it did its best impersonation of a Blue Angels flier, trying to get me off with spins and dips. I slid down the long neck, but didn't release my hold.

"Keep that shit up and I'll be throwing up all over you," I warned it.

I cracked an eye to see the glittering green, gold, and maroon beast give me the evil eye, its neck craned at an impossible angle.

"Wait, you understand me?" I asked, seeing intelligence in those purple eyes. The ride settled out immediately.

"I'm not moving. I let go, and there is nothing to stop you from dumping me."

The beast huffed, angling toward the ground at dangerous speed.

"I sure as hell hope you know what you are doing," I muttered, closing my eyes and covering my face as the branches snapped by in a painful blur.

The roar wrenched the air as powerful claws stopped our descent. I slipped off onto the ground with a thud, the world still spinning.

"That was awesome." Rolling to my side, I patted the beast's flank. It huffed at me.

"Okay," I began, stumbling slightly as I walked to its head; apparently, we were playing nice now. "So my dad said I had to name you to release my true and hopefully exceptionally deadly power." My voice dipped down, imitating my father's seriousness.

No response.

"How about Precious?"

The dragon breathed fire and I danced out of the way.

"Ouch! There is no need for that!"

I swear the damn thing smiled.

"Fine, no Precious, how about Asshole!"

I was prepared for the blast of inferno this time, ducking out of the way, laughing. I was so close to freeing my power and giving us a true fighting chance against the Fae. He or she could try scorching me all day.

I sat on my butt, folding my legs up and pressing a finger against my lips. "Okay seriously, want to give me any hints?"

The beast lumbered down, waiting. "Did you just roll your eyes at me?" I accused. There was that damn half smile again.

"OLIVIA!" Logan bellowed, coming to a screeching halt in front of us. "What the fuck are you doing?" he demanded.

"We've reached an agreement. It only tries to kill me when I give it a name it doesn't like."

"You're insane," he groaned, sitting next to me, naked, his clothing destroyed by his earlier rapid shift. I wasn't sure if we had packed additional clothing for him or not. By now we really should have known to.

"You already said that," I helpfully reminded him.

"What have you tried so far?" he asked, his eyes glued to the impressive, deadly predator.

"Precious and Asshole."

Logan looked at me. "Now why on Earth wouldn't she like those names?"

"Huh, you think she is a girl, too?"

"Why else would the damn thing chase us, then sit here waiting to be named? A male would still be trying to kill you."

The dragon huffed and smoke curled out her nostrils.

"I think we are both offended."

Using his hand to bat the smoke away, he coughed, "Female, definitely female."

"What about Fluffy?" I asked with a smile.

I shoved Logan to the side as the fire blasted over our head.

"You knew she wasn't going to like that one!" he accused me.

I laughed and nodded.

"What are you doing?" Garrick yelled, the crashing behind us announcing the arrival of our companions.

"Why haven't you bound the dragon yet?" my dad asked.

Fluffy stood up, like a cat arching its back.

"Like with rope?" I asked.

My father looked between us, terrified and shocked.

I shrugged, "We've come to an understanding. I'm trying to name her now."

"You don't know how to BIND a dragon? It could easily destroy you, end you without thought. Why didn't you tell me—"

I stopped him there. "I have no magical knowledge. You know this. Granted, going in without much of a plan wasn't brilliant on my part, but here we are, figuring it out." Like I always do, like I always have without you. I didn't add that last thought aloud. But it hung there unsaid between us, wounds I never even knew I carried refusing to heal.

I shrugged, not meeting Logan's gaze as my mood turned sour. "Let's focus on the positive, shall we? I've ridden said dragon, and I'm working on the naming now. We have an agreement."

"You have ridden her?" The Magician asked, apparently also agreeing it was a female.

"Yep, she set me down so I didn't puke on her."

My dad threw his hands up as Doyle lumbered into the clearing, bowing before the great she-beast.

"Okay, so seriously, a name." I tapped my foot, watching those eerie orchid eyes watching my own.

I smiled. "Emerald."

Logan jumped to the side, but I held my ground.

The dragon nodded once.

"Nice." I rubbed my hands together, turning to my father. "Okay, I did it, how is my magic released?"

He stared at me, open-mouthed. "You make the dragon do it, that's why you have to name her true name—to control her."

"I don't want to control her. I just want to unlock my magic and leave."

The dragon peered over my shoulder at my father. Can't lie, that was a weird sensation.

"Why don't I just ask? She understands us." I turned to Emerald, who was way too close for comfort.

"Hey Emerald, can you unlock my power?"

I swear she fucking grinned before her jaws clamped down on my shoulder.

I screamed, trying to pull back, "I really should have gone with Asshole!" I breathed through the pain. There was no headshaking, no death rattle, and while her sharp teeth hurt, they weren't going any deeper. For being in a dragon's mouth, I had to admit, I felt relatively safe.

"Stop moving!" my father demanded. "Logan, leave it, she's fine." I couldn't see much, what with a giant fucking lizard head blocking my view.

Her saliva dripped into the wound like acid. I screamed in earnest, bucking against her. Evidently, my dad had a strange idea of "fine." As quickly as the pain had started, though, it vanished and I sagged to the ground.

I cracked an eye, looking for safety, looking for Logan. I was so used to him coming to my rescue and wrapping me up in his powerful arms. Doyle was holding him back as my father watched me expectantly.

"I don't feel anything," I told him sadly. Maybe I wasn't as powerful as everyone thought.

Emerald dipped her head down to nudge me.

You are powerful, little one. I have chosen to unlock your power due to your laughter. Never in my many years has a Magician's child fought with such creativity and humor at death. I will take you at your word and leave now.

I blinked at her dumbly. "You can talk!" I scolded. She smiled, yeah, I was one hundred percent certain that toothy mouth was smiling at me.

Standing, I turned back to my father and Logan as the world spun. I hit my ass hard with a groan, dark spots coating my vision. My father's face came into a hazy focus as he instructed, "Don't fight it."

I slurred a response; what it was, not even I could tell you.

Chapter 10

Logan watched Olivia intently in the rearview mirror.

"She is fine," her father reassured him yet again.

Logan's view cut to The Magician's sea green eyes, mirrors of Olivia's own.

"You know that for certain?" Logan demanded.

Garrick shifted in the passenger seat. "Red light," he muttered.

Logan's glare cut to the Master Vampire as he braked. He glanced at Olie again and back to the street in front of him. His fingers tapped against the steering wheel.

"You should have warned us," Logan growled.

Her father sighed, "I didn't know."

"Oh, that's not what you should tell him." Garrick pushed himself against the car door.

Logan growled.

"Hush, I'm fine."

Logan's gaze jerked to Olivia as she pushed into a sitting position, rubbing her head. She reached a hand between the seats, pulling his right arm closer so she could awkwardly snuggle. Her forehead against the side of his bicep was heated.

"You're burning up."

She groaned, pulling him closer. It was an awkward angle to be sure, but the contact eased him. "I know."

"What do you need?" he asked softly.

She mumbled, her head drooping. Logan bent his arm, twisting even more to hold her head against his skin.

"Tell me your plan to make this better," Logan demanded of everyone.

"Nothing. She must walk this journey on her own." Her father's voice was soft.

"If this leaves lasting harm, it will become my personal mission to cause you pain. Every. Single. Day."

Garrick huffed, "You get that from Olivia?"

Logan snarled and Garrick quickly looked away.

...

It wasn't red, thank the fucking gods, but it wasn't my world, the real world. I looked around with a sinking feeling. It was Fae.

What. The Fuck. Can I not catch a fucking break, without it being closely followed by more horrid shit?!

I looked down at myself. The black dress was back. I tipped my head back, seeing a perfectly blue sky. I didn't feel panicked, which couldn't be right. I should have been downright terrified, peeing all over that gorgeous dress, instead I was calm. Perfectly tranquil, and pissed.

"It's your power."

I turned, seeing an ice throne and a pale Queen looking haggardly down upon me.

"I thought Luharposn took you?"

She shook her head. "He took my twin, my half, the flame to my ice. I am dying without her."

I squared my gaze to her. "I need my magic to fight him."

She nodded. "That is true, and even then I fear it won't be enough."

Now was probably a great time to negotiate for all kinds of shit.

"Why am I here?" Still needed to unlock my power.

"This world is fluid. It creates, moves, and is easy to manipulate." She drew a ragged breath. "I assume you are here since it's also the birthplace of all and it will be easier here to destroy the barrier to your magic."

"Any ideas on that?"

"Imagine it, will it, be it."

"Cryptic much?"

"Make haste, I fear we do not have much longer. The death of the Queens will put all of us at risk."

"Why?"

"Without us, we lose the balance of the Fae. They will be like dogs fighting for this world and will not hesitate to enslave yours and others for their own gain."

I couldn't disagree with anything there. "What is Luharposn's plan?"

"Kill the Queens, were you not paying attention?" she drawled.

"How does one kill a Fae?"

"There are a few different ways. Poisoning with enough iron, inescapable bindings, but the simplest is to keep us away from our world. We need the energy here for survival. Without it, we perish."

"How long?"

She shrugged, her bony shoulders causing her dress of icicles to tinkle against her ashen skin. "Time moves differently across our worlds. I know she is weak, and dying. Therefore, I am dying and our kingdoms will crumble."

"Yeah, can't say I have a shit to give about that. But you know, the whole enslaving my world, that I have issues with."

Her icy gaze pierced me. I shrugged, "Keeping it real. Alright, imagine it, will it, be it." I repeated her words. I closed my eyes, searching inside myself. Memories sprung to life, and I sifted through them until I came to a solid wall. I searched up to no end, sent my energy sideways to the ends, not finding one. I pressed my hands against the rough grey wall in my mind and pushed.

It creaked, a crack forming. I shoved again, feeling my insides mirror the tearing, searing and ripping. I locked my jaw, flexing my hands into fists. Playtime was over, the time for being nervous and uncertain stopped now.

This, what lay behind this wall, was my heritage. My birthright, and even though I fucking suck with change, this would protect my makeshift family.

I slammed my fists against the wall in rapid succession, screaming until it crumbled beneath my onslaught. I fell to my knees, the moment perfectly contained while I drew a slow breath. Before me was a magnificent sight, pinpricks of light, surrounded with pink, merging to red, wine, purple and blues. My next breath was in awe, Mine.

I stood up and walked into my birthright.

...

She came to, screaming in his arms. Light poured out of her eyes, her body vibrating, her voice not her own. He held on through the searing pain and scalding light. Turning his face away as her body convulsed, he held on. She was his heart and soul, nothing would take her from him.

...

I groaned, rolling over and into Logan, burying my aching head.

"We have to find the Fae Queen," I mumbled into his chest.

"Go back to bed."

"She's dying,"

124

"And?"

"Her twin said it would lead to the enslavement of our world."

"She might be scaring you to get you to help," Logan reminded me, pulling me closer, easily accepting my pain-laden words.

I shifted against him, slipping my head onto his shoulder, loving his strong arm around my waist. I sighed contentedly.

"Where did you go?" he whispered, the mate bond conveying his worry and fear.

"To Fae, or Fairy, whatever the hell they call their world." I pushed up on an elbow, looking down at this shirtless wonder I now called my own, the sheer masculinity of finely sculpted muscles almost distracting me from my next sentence. "I did it, though," I told him proudly.

He shifted positions, running his thumb down my cheek and over my bottom lip. I nipped at him playfully.

"Are you healed?" he asked seriously.

I gave him a wicked smile, "I could use some help with that."

Logan ran warm hands over my body, and while I knew part of his exploration was to be sure I was, indeed, alright, I didn't mind. His touch grounded me and drove all my worries away. I just wanted to be lost in his touch and forget about the daunting task in front of us.

Warm hands cupped my ass and I shifted to straddle him, glad for our lack of clothing. He slipped into me like he had always belonged there and a contended sigh eased past my lips. Letting my head fall, exposing my neck, I rocked to a rhythm I knew well. He didn't stay prone long, expertly changing our positions.

I smiled up at him, capturing his lips against my own, breathing in his scent, his strength, and mostly his love. Down my neck he trailed love bites as he lifted my left leg over his hip. My hands lightly running over his sides, I closed my eyes, awash in emotions. That's when I saw it.

Currents, threads of energy trailing from Logan to me, thin and bright. I pulled from him, the cords absorbing into me, healing the places that hurt.

"Hey," he whispered, "you okay?"

I snapped my eyes open; all of that could wait. I smiled up at him. "Perfect."

Chapter 11

Someone was banging on our door. I groaned, looking up at the noonday sun that slipped around the closed curtains.

Logan stepped out of the shower, a towel slung around his hips.

"Olivia!" Garrick bellowed.

I groaned, dropping my head back into the soft down pillow.

"Go away!" I growled.

The door unlocking was not the way I wanted this to go.

"Logan," I whined.

"She's still resting," he stated firmly.

"Not anymore. You are going to want to see this."

Garrick barged in, resting thick, worn, leather-bound volumes on the circular breakfast table.

I pushed up to a seated position, noting my lack of clothing. Logan growled and tossed me one of his shirts. Easing it over the loves bites from earlier, I went to stand next to Garrick, the throbbing in my head almost gone.

"Declan found this," he explained.

"What is it?" I asked.

"Who's Declan?" Logan questioned, biting into an apple.

"Food?" I questioned in a whine.

He tossed me an apple, I caught it and tossed it back. I was aiming for his smirk, but he caught the apple.

"Food," I demanded.

"It's called fruit, and eating a few of them once a month wouldn't hurt you."

I made a face at him, turning back to Garrick.

"Who's Declan?" I asked.

"My new replacement, should anything happen to me. The other lad got tired of waiting for me to die or retire," Garrick stated with a shrug.

I laughed. "You, retire? HA!"

"Stranger things have happened, like a succubus mating the Alpha shifter," he reminded me. I rolled my eyes.

"Anyways, what Declan was able to find is that the Fae have an allergy to iron. It burns their skin, renders their magic dulled, gives them dastardly headaches.

"The Queen told me the same. Also, being apart from Fae for too long will kill them as well. What's made out of iron?" I asked.

"Everything," Garrick answered.

I blinked at him. "Ev-ery-thing," he repeated, turning to face me, resting his ass against the table. "Cars, nails, screws, pots, pans, anything with steel by default contains iron. Fireplace tools..." He drew a breath and smiled, "and bullets."

"How can the Fae possible plan on surviving here with so much iron?" I asked.

"They're not, are they?" Logan asked.

"No." Garrick drew a breath, bracing his hands on the table next to him.

I felt my short-lived happiness at unlocking my magic and finding ways to kill the Fae crushed.

"Declan believes the Fae will remake the world, just like Fairy."

I exhaled, "The humans would be enslaved." Whispering softly, I added, "We wouldn't fare much better."

Logan nodded. "Where is Declan now? I'd like to know where he thinks they are."

"I thought you'd say that. I have a vehicle waiting to take us to our headquarters here." Garrick turned, gathering his books.

I plucked one off the top. "Reading material," I shrugged, taking a bite of the apple, since it was apparently the only nourishment currently available.

Garrick rolled his eyes. "Be ready in thirty."

I grunted, taking another bite as he swept out of the room.

"What are we going to do with your father and Doyle?" Logan asked, still reclined against the small kitchenette.

I sighed, sitting and setting both the text and apple down.

"I don't know. In a perfect world, I'd have time to learn the ins and outs of my newfound powers so that I could come in guns blazing against the Fae, but—"

"We lack the time," Logan finished.

I gave him a long-winded sigh. "That's what you were going to say," he defended.

"Yeah, but I was going to say it. When you say it, I instantly want to disagree."

"But you do agree."

"Do we have any actual food?" I grumbled.

"No, but go shower and I'll call for room service."

"How did you get two apples and nothing more?"

"I went to breakfast, it's now lunch. I didn't expect you to be awake before anything else went bad."

I grunted at his sensibleness; apparently I was spoiling for a fight.

"Do you want company?" Logan yelled at me.

I flipped him off.

"That wasn't a clear answer."

I opened the door, I had just slammed.

"That's a fucking clear answer," I grumbled with a smile.

...

Tossing my hair into a wet bun, I scarfed down the food on the rolling cart. Logan tossed a napkin at me, I made a face while overstuffing my mouth.

He rolled his eyes with a smile.

I stared longingly at the rest of the eggs, toast, and waffles.

"Are you still hungry?" Logan asked, picking my bag up off the bed.

"No, but it seems a shame to waste," I pouted.

He laughed. I noted that all the meat had been devoured. He handed me the worn text Garrick had left behind.

Time for a crash course in Fae.

My father was waiting in the corridor, arms crossed, foot tapping, annoyance and frustration oozing off of him.

"You cannot leave," he hissed, matching my quick pace. Logan fell behind us, creating the illusion of privacy.

"I don't have a choice," I responded.

"Olivia, daughter," he pleaded, pulling my arm to stop and turn me toward him. "You have unleashed massive power inside of you, power not even I know what will do. We must take time to understand it and teach you how to use it."

"Look, I get it, I want that, but I have a rogue Fae running around with the Queen of Fae, who is dying. If I don't get her back to Fae"—how the fuck was I doing that, by the way—"all those unruly fuckers come over to our world and we all die."

His sea green gaze searched my own, finding no compromise. "This is dangerous. If you use too much energy or tap into your lifeforce, you will die."

"I repeat, we all die. Give me the Cliffs Notes on how not to."

He sighed, rubbing his forehead before turning to slowly walk down the hall. I followed, coming up beside him.

"A lifetime of magic reduced to a few simple sentences," he muttered, running a hand over his stubbled face.

He sighed with added force. "Magic is malleable, you can form it into whatever you can believe. There is a great deal stored within you, but you can also pull from the elements." He stopped, putting a hand on my arm. "Do not ever, ever, pull from your lifeforce. Drain that and you are dead. Immortal or not."

I nodded, "I'll be careful." I squeezed his hand on my arm.

"See that you are," he whispered, moisture pooling in his eyes.

I cleared my throat. "I need you—"

"Back at the manor." He cleared his throat, looking away. "I'll keep them safe."

I nodded. "Garrick said the Fae are dangerously allergic to iron. Buy whatever you need to ward the property. Be sure Mercer brings Mindy, even if he won't stay himself."

"I'll protect them, daughter. Just as I would you."

"Thank you." I turned and walked away.

That seemed to be my father's new job title, defender of my children, since I was out and about saving the freaking world. I never used to mind doing it, but I did now. I wanted—what I wanted didn't matter, what I needed to do was kill the Fae and send the Queen back to her world. Easy peasy.

...

Declan met us at Garrick's temporary office.

"I am shocked you work here," I told him.

Garrick raised an eyebrow at me as our steps echoed off the soup pantry's bare interior.

"I don't."

Logan chuckled.

"What happened with your magic?" Garrick asked. "I never did ask."

"It's unlocked. I can feel it inside. I'm hesitant to try anything, though."

"Your father?"

"I sent him home to the kids."

Garrick stopped. "Just to be clear, you are running around, unchecked and untrained, with heavens-know-how-much power pumping through your veins?"

"Yep," I confirmed.

He looked to Logan. "And you agreed to this?"

Logan shrugged. We had discussed it, it seemed to be our best plan.

"I'll figure it out, the same way I did being a succubus, the same way I do everything."

Garrick opened a door into the main room. The water-stained, peeling drywall of the room we had just walked through was replaced by freshly hung and painted charcoal gray walls. Black desks were dotted around the room with various vampires occupying the seats. Their speed gave them away, fingers flying over keyboards as they spoke into their sleek headsets.

A dark-haired man straightened from speaking to one of the vamps, adjusting his finely pressed suit before turning to lay his gaze on us.

"Declan, this is Olivia and Logan."

He nodded, clearly unimpressed. His hazel gaze flicked over Logan and me before dismissing us. I tilted my head; certainly an acknowledgement wasn't too much to ask? I felt Logan sizing him up. Declan was shorter, smaller and didn't have the sheer muscle capacity Logan did. While he was taller than me, he didn't exude the threatening energy I had come to expect from a powerful Supernatural. A slow throbbing built behind my temples. Taking a step toward Logan, I braced a hand against my head.

"What's wrong?" he breathed against my ear.

I could see them. The thin and numerous threads that wrapped around Declan, the colors spanning the rainbow, and I felt, more than knew, that each one had a specific purpose. Easing an exhale, I was debating how rude it would be for me to pluck them off.

"Don't," Declan's voice warned.

I struggled to open my heavy lids. He was regarding me warily.

"You never had powers before," he stated.

I grunted as Logan eased my weight down into a couch, realizing we had moved rooms during my little blackout.

"She does now," Logan answered. I didn't need to look at him to know he was staring down Declan. I could feel him carefully evaluating the man's power after his initial dismissal. We both had missed something.

"What are you?" I asked. Jerry didn't throw that level of complex threads. I hadn't studied my father while he was doing magic, but this power just felt different.

Declan regarded me for a moment, looking down his perfectly sculpted nose as my head throbbed again. I dropped it into my hands, easing out a breath.

"I'd prefer not to say," was his cryptic answer.

I opened my eyes to glare at him. "What are you?" Logan asked again.

"We won't be asking a third time," I added. "I don't have time for games."

Declan looked to Garrick for help, who offered only, "If you plan on ruling after me, dealing with these two will be your responsibility."

Declan looked back to me and I swear I saw threads dancing in his eyes. "Gearing up for a fight?" I asked him, the adrenaline clearing my mind. "We can go, but before we do, know that my magic is new and untrained, and I have zero problems with making Garrick replace you."

Garrick groaned my name, shaking his head. Logan's own need to dominate wasn't helping me stay rational, riding me along the mate bond.

"I'm not looking for a fight." Declan over-enunciated the syllables and I growled.

I narrowed my eyes, my normal and magical sights merging as sparks danced along his magical threads. "How do you know so much about the damn Fae, anyway?"

He adjusted his suit. "Again, I'd rather not say."

"Alright, that's it. You, me, and a sparring room. NOW!" I demanded.

"And what, if you win I spill all my secrets?" Declan asked with a laugh. He clearly didn't know who he was taunting.

"Nope, I don't want all your secrets, just for you to answer my questions."

"I don't have time to indulge your idle fantasies of beating me."

"Lords, Olivia, don't kill him," Garrick groaned.

"No guarantees."

I didn't get a sparring room. What I got was an empty pantry. I scanned the empty shelves, the wood rotting away, and picked out a few structurally intact places I was going to toss Declan's body against. Slipping out of my jacket, I ignored Logan's annoyed stare.

I don't like this. You can't sense what he is.

Normally I'd bluff, but since I had asked and Logan could read my mind, that response was void.

He's got magic, probably not used to using his body to physically respond to threats, and knows a whole shit ton about the Fae, I thought back.

Do you think he's a mole? Logan questioned.

I pondered the question, watching Declan speak with Garrick.

No, but he's hiding something and I'm going to find out what it is.

Declan turned to me then, still annoyed at my antics. Okay, so maybe challenging him to a fight was a little immature. I'm willing to admit that. I'm also willing to admit I needed him to know EXACTLY who he was dealing with. I took over a Council that was run so poorly it harmed more than helped; I wasn't above going after the Western Council if he thought he could run it the same way.

Besides, it did annoy me that I couldn't place exactly what he was. Granted, in a case of diluted blood, I had a harder time placing the exact origins of power, but if you haven't noticed, I'm a control freak.

"Let's go, princess, I have things to do," Declan said, standing six paces from me. His look of boredom was highly insulting.

I huffed. "Only one person calls me that," I told him, clearing the distance between us, "and it's not you."

He blocked the assault I laid into him, punch after uppercut, with a few well placed kicks. At least his look of boredom was gone.

Good, I was a contender, still.

A fake left followed by a right jab caught him under the chin, and I delighted in the flash of raw anger crossing his dark eyes, once he righted his head. Ha.

I felt more than heard Logan's groan, my love of smashing my fists into deserving flesh rushing through my veins.

Declan came at me, fists a blur as I blocked, my forearms bearing the brunt of his onslaught of anger. I smiled, the physical altercation forcing us both to breathe hard.

As suddenly as his assault began, it stopped. I stood up from my stance, ready to demand answers again, but a flick of his fingers had me pinned in place, my jaw locked shut.

Son of a bitch! I screamed at Logan.

Do you need me?

I took a breath, my eyes attempting to narrow at the cocky asshole Declan.

Not yet.

Not ever going to fight my battles for me, was the thought I hid. I needed to get myself out of this jam. I did start it, after all.

Opening my second sight, I looked at the olive cords of magic wrapped around my body. Unlike the cords of magic I had encountered before, these resembled what I imagined my emotions looked like when I manipulated them—thicker, hardier. I could feel their weight on me. Plucking wasn't going to be an option.

Cutting, however, was.

Closing my eyes, I looked inside, something I hadn't bothered to do since my encounter with Emerald, the friendly fire-breathing dragon, and saw nothing. I was disappointed. I had expected massive, raw, untapped and writhing power. Even my father had said I had a great capacity.

What I got was a vastness. With a sigh, I sent my senses out. Perhaps I could pull magic into myself, like I did with emotions. Problem: I wasn't touching anything.

Except my feet were, I realized, sending my awareness there. The concrete beneath me pulsed with emotions. This was new. My head tipped back as sensations swarmed me—desperation, heartache and hopelessness. I drew it all into me, coiled it the same way I always had.

Then I touched Declan's cords, feeling his supreme confidence. I almost felt bad about what I was about to do. Almost. I wrapped the hopelessness around his olive cords, infusing it, blending it. I watched his colors change, until the darkness I handled with ease took over. An ebony-colored disease, spreading back to the host.

"Shit," Declan hissed. I heard the worry. He may have had some fancy magic, but I was fighting dirty. I know, I know, nothing new here.

Swiftly speeding down the cords, the darkness grew, swirling until it reached Declan. I opened my eyes, leveling my gaze with his.

He clutched his heart, fingers pressed tightly into his perfectly starched white shirt. He took a ragged breath, fear playing over his features. I took a step forward, his cords now my own, obeying me.

"You are mine." I didn't recognize my own voice.

"Olivia," Declan tried.

I raised my chin and he was silent, bowing his head.

A dark chuckle slipped past my lips, seductive and dangerous. I was losing myself.

Olivia.

I took another step forward, more threads moving through me. They were all mine. All of them belonged to me. My pets, my pawns.

Olivia.

I hissed at the intrusion, turning to the source.

"Olivia," Logan's rich voice washed over me.

I blinked at him, still not releasing Declan.

"Olivia." Logan stepped toward me, eyes stern. "Enough."

Raw power washed over me again. I could bring him to his knees, make him worship me.

No, a small voice whispered. Not my wild lion.

And that's what it took to crack the magic's hold on me.

"Shit," I whispered, turning to see Declan wheezing through the pain.

I cleared the distance between us. "Shit, shit, shit." Laying my hands over his, still clutching his heart, I pulled what I had pushed into him.

He drew a clear breath, his eyes focusing on me. "What, the fuck, was that?"

It was my turn to release a shuttering breath. "Apparently, all my old tricks have been magnified. Although being able to pull emotions from inanimate objects is new."

Declan shook his head at me.

"Back to you. What are you?" I asked, backing up so he could stand.

"A Druid," he finally answered.

I blinked at him. "Like a mage?" I asked, having no idea what the fuck that meant.

"No, my magic functions differently, faster and more potent."

"So you are a jacked up mage? Like a Magician?"

Declan recovered from his shock. "Yes, in a way. I suppose we are similar."

"How do you know so much about the Fae?" I asked.

He shifted uncomfortably. "My kind has had dealings with them for a very, very long time."

"Eww."

He shrugged.

I nodded. "What other magical species are going to come out of the fucking woodwork?" I groaned, turning to Logan.

I cleared the distance between us, wrapping my arms around his thick neck. "Thank you," I whispered into his ear as he bent down to hold me closely.

"Mermaids, unicorns, and now Druids," I muttered into his neck.

Logan was calming his inner beast, so while I wanted to pull away from our public display of affection, I stayed trapped by his strong arms.

...

Back in their makeshift office, I let Logan take the lead. I kept slipping into my second sight and analyzing everything. It was driving Declan insane, or at least highly annoying him, from the narrowed-eyes looks he was sending me.

"You think they are in Oregon?" Logan repeated.

"Possibly. The Fae have been sighted there before, and we've also had other indicators. Regardless, I'll be able to cast a spell to lead us to them there."

"What other indicators?" I asked.

"The number of unusual cases for us has doubled since your incident with the talking tree. Not to mention the greenery would appeal to the Fae."

"The cool weather would appeal to the Queen as well," I muttered.

"Which Queen?" Logan asked.

"Mine," I answered with malice. "Let's go to Oregon. I need to kill my mother."

Chapter 12

Logan took care of the arrangements, and I was soon sitting and staring at the back of Declan's head in our private jet.

"Coming up in the world, Olivia," Garrick said, sitting next to me. Logan was speaking with the pilot.

I huffed an answer, "I prefer to drive."

Garrick laughed, "I'm shocked we aren't."

I shrugged. "Logan prefers to fly, says it's more efficient."

"It is."

Again, I shrugged. "What's wrong?" Garrick asked.

I turned and looked into his brown eyes, so much running through my mind. I wasn't sure I could win this one. How would I tell my father I'd killed my mother? Could I really overcome my fear and horrid memories of Luharposn? My worst nightmares had come to life, and I missed the simpler days of rogue vampires and shifters gone beast.

"Just wondering if I should charge you for taking care of this problem," was what I said.

Garrick laughed. "You are the root of this problem. Had you not almost died…"

I winced, touching my scars. "Don't remind me. Life was simpler when I thought I was lab created."

Garrick nodded, "Strange times, indeed."

I nodded.

...

We were landed and in rental cars, following a "hunch" Declan had about the Fae's location.

"I don't think I beat him enough, he's still keeping secrets," I told Logan.

"Are we even going to talk about what your magic is now capable of?" he asked.

I huffed, "It's potent."

"And untrained."

I shrugged, "Since when do we ever have the luxury of time?"

He sighed, "True." He took my hand resting on the center console, intertwining our fingers. I relaxed into my seat. The tension in my shoulders eased, the gut-churning fear calmed. I turned to look at him.

"You gotta admit, it's a neat trick."

He shook his head, a caramel lock dusting his brow. I reached up with my free hand to brush the hair back.

"Your eyes turned black again."

I sat back. "I wonder why. That must be due to my succubus side. My father's eyes never turn black."

Logan nodded, "I'd assume so."

"So many unanswered questions as to who I am. I thought I knew it all," I said softly.

Logan squeezed my hand.

"Return the Queen of the Fae, kill the bad guys, be home for dinner."

I nodded, not sharing his optimism.

"I think we should bring The Magician and Doyle out for this."

"Agreed," Logan said. I was surprised he didn't add an 'I told you so.'"

...

We stopped alongside a thick canopy of trees, which so far was all I had seen of Oregon. I pulled my leather jacket closer around me, discreetly touching all my hidden weapons.

Logan stretched, coming around from the driver's side. His desire to run was evident in the longing look he gave the wooded landscape.

"Go run," I told him with a shooing motion.

"We need to climb down to the bottom before I can perform the tracking spell," Declan stated, slinging a designer bag across his shoulders.

"You need one of those," I told Logan, almost not laughing.

Declan leveled an annoyed look at us, now both laughing.

"Olivia, no crossbow?" Garrick asked.

I rolled my eyes at him. "No, I'm packing enough heat, thank you."

Logan filled his lungs again with the crisp air.

"Seriously, don't make me tell you again."

Logan smiled, chucking his pants at me. "Do you want a purse to carry those in?" he asked with a laugh.

I just rolled my eyes, tossing the still warm denim over my shoulder and tamping down my libido, which was enjoying the scents his clothing was giving off so damn close to my nose.

A wet nose brushed against my ass and I batted at him.

...

Logan couldn't resist teasing Olie in this form. He could smell her desire and it heightened his own for her. So much had been dropped on her, yet she took it in stride, never backing down, never breaking down. She was just bent on saving the world, again.

He noticed a new dimension to her scent, a darkness that gave him pause. He knew Olivia hated the demon reference attached to her kind, but he was wondering if there wasn't some truth to it. He would be interested to understand the scale and scope of her mother's power, and whether the spell The Magician had placed on Olivia in her infancy had hidden all of her innate magical abilities.

Down they trekked through the lush greenery, and Logan darted off to the side, sensing something.

...

Asshole was chasing rabbits. Seriously.

Well, I assumed it was a rabbit. Some furry creature to kill and eat. He was definitely brushing his teeth before he kissed me again.

I huffed a sigh. "How much longer?" I complained.

Neither Declan nor Garrick bothered to answer me. Assholes, the lot of them.

After a long, humid hike, my leather was chafing and I was complaining in epic proportions.

"I will spell you silent," Declan threatened.

I laughed, "We all saw how well your spells did against me. Nope."

More walking. More hiking. More complaining.

"We've arrived, princess."

"I told you. Do. Not. Call. Me. That. If you make me tell you again, I will remove your tongue," I told him, looking around at the circle of ferns.

Declan swallowed.

"I get the impression you aren't threatened very often," I observed.

"Not by someone who can follow though," Garrick said with a laugh.

I smiled, smugly, not going to lie.

Declan narrowed his gaze at us.

"So, what now?"

"Shouldn't you call your dog?"

"He's a lion and no, he's hunting something."

"How can you tell?"

I tapped my temple. "We speak without words."

"The mating?" Garrick asked.

I nodded, flexing my hands on my hips.

Declan took off his man purse, and with a tap of his foot against the grass-covered center of the clearing, an earthen pedestal pushed up from the dirt.

"Was that always there?" I asked, circling around the perfectly round, waist-high structure.

"No, our type of magic allows us to create and pull from the world around us. I wanted a place to set my tools and I got it."

"Interesting," I mused. "So what supplies do you need?"

"I needed the blood of Luharposn. He was gravely injured here," he murmured.

"How long ago?" I asked. How long had the Fae been bouncing between the realms? How much damage had they done to this world?

"Two, maybe three hundred years ago," he answered, carving symbols into the ground. "Fresh blood wouldn't require the ceremony."

"Good to know," I muttered, walking the circle. I squinted out into the thick foliage. Logan was stalking something. His beast didn't like the magic the druid was wielding, which was funny since he himself transformed because of magic.

I turned back to Declan, tuning out his chanting and tuning into his magic. He was wielding shades of green, pulling from the earth, searching for a spot of red so old it had become one with the earth again.

Slowly, more slowly than our trek down, he extricated the substance he sought, careful not to disturb it. With sweat beading his brow, Declan deposited the blood into a worn golden chalice, encrusted with precious gems.

Blowing out a breath, he opened a paper map. "Hold this," he instructed me. I moved, holding it up, blocking my view of him. I could see where this was going. Whatever he did next would indicate in some way where Luharposn and the Queens were.

The paper trembled in my hands, heating up.

"Gah! Warning would have been nice." I straightened my arms out, holding the smoldering paper away from me. While it was hot, it was smokeless—small favors.

The heat burned the paper at the center in a perfect circle, the edges blackened and spreading. I watched the growing hole, wondering if it would deviate from the perfect circle. Certainly, if it found where Luharposn was holing up with the Queens it would. I kept my doubt at bay, looking up and into Declan's perfectly sculpted scowl.

Something was wrong.

Where was Logan?

The paper burned right to the edges in my hands. I shook them out, looking down at the dying embers and ash in the dense vegetation.

"Maybe he isn't in the U.S.?" Garrick offered.

Declan looked at the podium, back to the burned map, and then at Garrick.

Dread began seeping into my gut. I pulled my gun.

"Olivia, please do not kill Declan."

I gave voice to my suspicions. "Something is wrong."

"It is." Declan turned to survey our surroundings.

Garrick, not one to be fazed by much, followed our intent gazes. "What do you think it is?" he asked.

"I don't know, but we need to find Logan." I sent out my awareness, searching for his silent ass.

No, came his gentle whisper, followed by resignation and regret and a stone-cold commitment to die in order to keep me safe.

"Motherfucker, you do NOT get to make those kinds of choices," I said both aloud and in my head.

Language, came his soft reply.

I was moving, not giving a shit if Declan and Garrick followed me. I stowed my gun, finding I actually had more confidence in my unstable and potent magic. I wanted Luharposn to be here. I wanted to rip him apart, cell by miserable cell. But what I wanted more was my mate back.

"Olivia, are you sure this is wise?" Garrick asked me, masking his uncertainty. Neither of us liked the Fae very much.

"Go back, Garrick, one of us needs to survive this for the Council."

"I'm insulted you think I would run from danger," was his only response. I rolled my eyes. I hadn't expected him to turn back, but it was worth a shot. When he complained later, I could always remind him of this moment. Pending we survived.

Forcing my mind away from that miserable train of thought, I plowed through the undergrowth, annoyed by it all and giving thought to burning it all away. Aside from the problems of announcing my presence and possibly wasting magic, I still wasn't sure of my capacity. And all that greenery actually was really pretty.

Flexing my newfound skills, I reached out to brush my hand against a tall redwood tree, feeling a deep-seated peace and a new flavor of magic I had never experienced before. I pulled more, enjoying the feeling to my core.

I wondered what it would do. My thoughts were on destruction, but I supposed healing might be another avenue I was capable of.

I liked destruction, death and mayhem better. I wondered which part of my heritage I got that from.

Consumed in my own thoughts and intently following the trail of Logan, I wasn't paying attention as well as I should have been. I missed the subtle change in front of my face, the lines of intricately woven power of pure ebony.

"Olivia! NO!" Declan screamed.

Too late, my next step took me directly into those dark tendrils, unmasking the scene that had been so carefully hidden from me.

Shadowy cords reached out to wrap around my waist, lifting me up above Luharposn, whose skull face grinned smugly, fire dancing along his jawbone and eyes.

"Four, so good to see you again," he rumbled.

"Release him." I didn't remember infusing my voice with magic, but damn if it didn't sound different.

Nothing in Luharposn's face gave away shock, but his hesitation in moving me did.

I wasn't going to repeat myself. Ignoring the magic at my waist, I sent my awareness to Logan, focusing on him. Luharposn was killing him, slowly tightening the coils around his lion form.

"Hmmm." I cruised inside the threads, absorbing the learning as I did so. "There it is." With a pluck I shredded the hold he had. Easily.

I fell, landing on my feet. I hadn't touched the magic holding me aloft and I didn't really care where it had gone. I was already moving to Logan, examining him with my second sight. All his ribs were crushed, his lung punctured by one of them, his internal organs a mess. I pushed out a trapped breath, hesitation and fear trying to force me into doing nothing.

I could hear Garrick and Declan screaming and pounding against the bubble Luharposn had made. Sending my awareness out, I felt Luharposn's uncertainty. But I cared for none of it. I only cared for my lion, dying in front of me.

Using my recently pulled calming energy, I placed my hands above his side, careful not to add more pain to his already labored breathing. Closing my eyes, I hummed slightly, or perhaps that was the magic humming. Either way, without much thought or command, it traveled from my stores down my arms, into my hands, and easily into Logan's body.

I carefully examined the energy, realizing it was sentient. I wasn't controlling anything, I had asked and it had responded. That should make a control freak like me uneasy, but it didn't. Perhaps that was always how my manipulation of emotions had worked.

Again, not what I cared about at the moment. I watched Logan's side rebuild itself, bones snapping back into place, soft tissue repaired. He lifted his head to look at me, shocked.

How did you do that? His voice returned to its usual rich timbre, instantly setting my heart at ease.

I wiggled my fingers at him. "Magic, darling,"

He chuffed an answer, carefully standing, shaking his thick, russet coat. He turned those gorgeous caramel eyes away from me and onto Luharposn with a growl.

"What are you?" Luharposn whispered.

"Really?" I asked, taking a step toward him. "I thought you of all people would know."

His silence was annoying. "Where are the Queens?" I demanded, tired of these games.

"Somewhere you'll never find them."

I groaned.

I hijacked his murky tendrils, wrapping them thickly around his legs and middle, squeezing for good measure.

I felt his resistance, his attempt to take back what I had stolen. His attacks were minimal, and my relief at being able to contain him immense. My greatest fear, neutralized. Score one for the abandoned hybrid.

Reaching for the walls of the bubble, I gave a tendril a spearhead end, punching it through. My ears popped and I heard Garrick and Declan fall, unprepared for the sudden disappearance of the barrier.

Declan was at my side in a moment, quickly using his own magic to take in what was happening. He clearly had some opinions on the matter, but kept them to himself.

"Now again, where are the Queens?" I asked. Luhaposn sneered.

I sighed, "I'm open to ideas on how to torture him."

Declan smiled. "I've got this."

"Oh, do share."

He laughed, "Secrets are meant to be kept."

"Party pooper," I groaned. I had not beaten him enough.

"Just hold him—" He paused. "With ... his own magic." He shook his head in disbelief, walking slowly to the tall and disgusting Fae struggling against my/his own hold. He had created the bonds well.

"He can pull information from a mind," Garrick whispered close to my ear.

I nodded, watching Declan reach a hand tentatively over to Luharposn, who snapped white teeth at his fingers. I wrapped my own tendrils around his mouth and the fire in his eyes roared to life.

I laughed. Logan leaned against me, checking my mental faculties. I wasn't being overwhelmed like I had been many times with the emotions I pulled. I wondered if since I had pulled from such a pure source, the repercussions would be different. I just felt calm and happy.

Happy I could defend my family. Happy I could eliminate the threat of the Fae. Happy my life was coming together again. Yes, I had lost Grams, and while I would always love her and miss her, this life was pretty amazing as well.

143

Luharposn screamed, and it was a beautiful sound my soul rejoiced in.

"How much pain do you want him in before I kill him?" Declan asked. Oh yeah, we were going to be friends after this.

"As much as you got," I answered, smiling wickedly, meeting his hazel gaze.

After Luharposn had screamed and writhed and begged, Declan took his hand away with a nod, sweat dotting his brow. "I have it, I know where they are."

He is Anna's father, Logan said to me.

He was, I answered, pulling my gun and shooting Luparhosn between the eyes.

He dropped, only my magic keeping him upright. I waited a moment, feeling his soul leave his body, taking its last breath before pulling out of his magic. It disappeared, his body turning to ash before our eyes. Tears welled in my eyes at that horrible chapter in my life ending, finally.

I blinked them back, because badass bitches do NOT cry.

Logan nudged my hand, privy to all my emotional turbulence. I fisted my fingers in his mane, wanting to wrap my arms around his neck and bury my face into him, but I didn't. It wasn't over. I still had shit to sort out.

WE still have shit to sort out, he reminded me.

I nodded.

I don't suppose you still have my pants, he asked.

I groaned inside and aloud. I'm sure I can find them. Maybe, hopefully.

Garrick beat me to the punch, asking Declan, "What did you find?"

The druid in question shook his head. "The Fae Queen was not kidnapped. She orchestrated the entire thing."

"Well, shit." My responses, I know, are impressive.

"So I'm guessing she doesn't want to head back to Fae peacefully," I groaned.

"No," Declan confirmed.

"That doesn't make any damn sense. The Ice Queen said she and Fae were dying because her sister wasn't there. Why would she stay away?"

"It's possible she lied to you," Logan reminded me, having shifted back to his wonderfully naked human form. Too true, never trust a Fae. "What of the Succubus Queen?" he asked. Points to him for not referring to her as my mother.

Declan shook his head again. "The Fae Queen has her as well—used Luharposn to kidnap all of them from the red world."

We walked back toward our original site and hopefully the location of Logan's pants.

"Why would the Fae Queen want a Succubus Queen?" I muttered to myself, tromping through the undergrowth. What did my mother have that she could need?

I sighed, "We need to know more about the Fae Queens."

"They are a mystery in themselves. Nothing they have ever done makes any sense," Declan muttered.

"How old are you?" I asked.

"Older than your boyfriend," he muttered.

"Mate," Logan growled.

"You are the baby in this situation, Olivia, by centuries," Garrick teased me.

I huffed, "Right, born powerful, die young. Anyways, we need Bob."

I ran right into the fucker and bounced on my ass.

"Dammit, Bob!" I screamed, hoping my anger covered up my surprise and fear.

"You called," was the only thing the short, leathery creature had to say.

"We need information on the Queens," Logan stated, helping me up.

"You didn't mention you had a Fae at your beck and call," Declan muttered.

"More like stalking me," I clarified.

"You're asking the wrong questions," Bob said, ignoring Declan.

"You lied about the other Queen," I accused him.

He shrugged, "How was I to know?"

"You are the Fae, known for having the sight," Declan stated, looking pointedly at the short-statured Fae.

I sighed. "What is happening in your world?" I tried again.

"Our world is dying, even if the Queen were to come back. It has begun, the end of a dynasty."

"No, nope, not ever going to happen. You fuckers are NOT coming to Earth."

"We already have. The iron content here consigns us to certain remote areas."

"Great, so you can kill, enslave, and torture off the grid." How had I fucking missed this?!?!?!

"Not all of the Fae are evil."

I laughed, "Right, that's a good one."

Bob stopped, looking at me earnestly. "We aren't."

I rubbed my forehead. "Prove it, show me where these Fae are. Tell me why the Queen is here and what she wants with my mother."

Bob's mouth formed a thin line. I was fairly certain he didn't have lips to speak of. His dark, large eyes bored into my own.

"I need permission."

"Then get it," I said, turning away from him and tromping through the ferns again.

I didn't bother looking, I knew he was gone.

"Was that wise?" Garrick asked.

"You and Logan have been hanging around each other too much. That's his line," I responded dryly. Why would the Ice Queen lie about the Fae needing to be in her world to survive? I groaned. Because a Queen isn't a Queen without someone to rule.

I turned to face Garrick and Logan. Declan was gathering his supplies now that we were back at our starting point. I noted with interest that the pedestal still stood. Intriguing. The magic had either stayed or made a permanent change. I'd have to ask more about that later.

"Okay, do you think that was wise?" Logan asked, slipping on his jeans.

I narrowed my eyes at him. "What other options do we have?"

"Kill them all?" Declan suggested.

I groaned. "I don't even know where they are, so unless you have another fancy way of figuring out where the hell the Fae have been stashing themselves, I think we need assistance."

"They will not bow to you," Declan added.

"Good, I hate that shit."

"He means they won't acknowledge you as their leader," Garrick clarified.

"Fine, what do I care? I just need to be sure they aren't fucking with the humans. As in killing. I actually don't care if they are sleeping with them. But the Fae are users, tricky and cruel. I don't need human causalities. Killing them all would be so much easier," I groaned.

I fucking hate the Fae.

Declan looked over as I dug my hands down my face, fingers pulling down my lids and dragging down the skin of my cheeks.

"That bad, eh?" Declan said.

I groaned, "Keep it up, you'll have to deal with these assholes as well."

"I do not fear the Fae," Declan said, trying the party line of the falsely brave.

I laughed, "You damn well should. Although," I sighed, "with these released powers I find myself more annoyed then fearful."

I shrugged. "Either way, we are burning daylight, let's get back to the cars."

We moved and the pedestal returned to the earth behind us. Declan didn't even look, the show off.

You are still learning. He was a beginner once, too.

I huffed, knowing Logan was right. In the heat of battle, my magic worked flawlessly. In calm and docile situations, nothing.

Give it time, Logan reminded me.

Time was a luxury I never had.

Chapter 13

The walk was silent back to the vehicles. We had climbed about halfway out of the ravine our journey had taken us into when Garrick and Logan both stopped.

"Vampires," they said as one.

"What the fuck do they want?" I asked, continuing to walk.

"Well, let's review, shall we?" Garrick began. "You killed off not one, but two Masters, not to mention a European Master, destroyed said Houses, literally and figuratively, gave Raphael a satellite home in St. Ann, and brushed off their attempts at talking. I do wonder why they are here."

I gave Garrick my best, unimpressed stare. How did he know all that?

"Oh, and Mal has your protection," he added. "Did I miss anything?"

I groaned and continued to hike out. "No point in keeping them waiting."

The vampires and I were not seeing eye to eye, another race whose numbers I felt okay about trimming down. Well, I suppose Logan and I already had. Hence our current issues. Killing Tate still felt wrong ... If he would have just sided with us. Then again, if he had, we'd probably be in an even bigger mess.

I gazed at my feet, plodding along the rich earth, pulling in more clean, calm energy before making the final bend. Logan and I led; this was our battle and we were going to enjoy it.

Blake.

"What the fuck?" I rocked back on my heels.

"How did you find us?" Logan asked. Yep, that was a much more productive question.

Blake shrugged, and I saw that his skin was sunken, dark circles etched under his washed-out complexion, his blue eyes diluted and unfocused.

I did feel sorry for him, wondering if perhaps he had sought me out to help him out of what appeared to be a loveless marriage, or perhaps life in general.

Either way, he is not your problem, Logan reminded me.

True. But killing him would give the unrest with the vampires more fuel.

"I —" he began, "I came to beg for your forgiveness." His voice was harsh, it didn't sound like him.

"What?" I asked, shocked.

"How did you find us?" Garrick asked.

Yes, back to the important questions.

"Tommy isn't the only one with impressive tech skills."

"Do. Not. Say. His. Name." It was my voice I didn't recognize now.

Blake took a step back. "Your eyes."

"How did you find us?" I demanded, infusing my words with compliance. At one point not so long ago, Blake had firsthand knowledge into my mind, my heart, and my emotions. Granted, it was nothing compared to the bond that Logan and I now shared.

Still, he had thawed my heart in ways I never dreamed possible, and paved the way for me to love Logan. There was a certain sentimentality attached to his memory, even if the vampire standing in front of me was a pale echo of that man. We had taken his House, his protection, and left him. Just left him.

He made his choices. You cannot save everyone, Olivia, especially from themselves.

Could you stop being right all the damn time? It's annoying.

I heard his answering chuckle.

We formed a semicircle around Blake, still not trusting the situation. Nothing was adding up. Was this another trap? A backup in case Luharposn didn't get the job done? How would they have known about my magic? I hadn't even known I could kill Luharposn.

A light rain misted upon us, yet still no one moved.

"K, forgiveness granted. Later," I said, crossing my arms.

He still didn't move. "You left me," he hissed.

I laughed. "You did the leaving. I just left you to your choices. I saved your ass enough. You chose Angelina, you get the consequences of it. I am not responsible for your poor choices."

"You granted Mal protection.'

"She deserved it," Logan rumbled.

"I could have saved Ginny." He was desperate. I saw it, I felt it. The raw emptiness and pain washed over me in powerful waves. I took a step back, holding a hand to my chest. That was new; my initial instinct was to block it, and I did. But after a moment, I absorbed it, sucking it into my reserves—these were powerful emotions that would be excellent to throw at an enemy.

149

Blake's shoulders straightened, shock widening his eyes, the piercing blue reappearing. "You never could do that before."

"I've got new tricks," I said with a shrug.

Logan turned to glare at me. I wasn't trying to help Blake and he knew that, but still I had, and that annoyed him to no end.

Blake shook his head sadly. "It doesn't matter. It's too late."

"What's too late? Stop talking in damn riddles!" I demanded, shoving raw power at him to tell me the damn truth. It wasn't very effective, not specific enough. It wasn't an emotion, just my overall annoyance with him.

Dammit.

Declan was the first to pick up that something wasn't right. Garrick closely followed.

"Olivia," Garrick whispered softly.

"What?" I growled.

"We are surrounded," Garrick said, not bothering to soften his voice again.

"Show yourselves!" demanded Declan, his voice echoing with magic.

Hundreds of vampires stepped forward. "Mother fucker," I hissed. "How the fuck did I miss this?"

"Magic," Declan said. "Powerful magic."

"We fighting our way out?" Logan asked, rolling his shoulders, smiling.

"The Vampire Council wants to see you, just meet with them," Blake implored.

"Oh that's a great idea, you back stabbing piece of shit!"

"We might as well go," Garrick said with a sigh. "As the mouthpiece of the Council, we request protection to, from, and during the meeting, that no harm shall befall any of us," he formally requested.

Blake nodded. "As the mouthpiece, I have been given permission to grant the protection of your party."

...

It was cramped in the backseat, sandwiched between Declan and Logan. Blake was giving Garrick instructions from the passenger seat. He wanted to drive, but Garrick wasn't having any of it.

"I can't believe they went through all this work for another damn meeting," I groaned.

"Stop plucking," Declan warned.

I sighed. "What is it?" I asked.

Yes, I had been picking at the thin threads of magic around him, although picking wasn't how I was viewing it. Examining, testing ... okay, plucking maybe.

"Glamour," Logan said.

I turned to look at him. "How do you know that?"

"He has a dual scent, that's glamour."

"And you didn't feel like sharing your findings before?"

"You didn't ask me."

"Oh, that's the game we are playing now?"

"It's not a game," he muttered, a smile creeping on his lips.

"It is, and you know I'm better at it than you." His grin split wide as he shrugged.

Another thirty minutes dragged by. "I have to pee," I complained.

"Hold it," Blake snapped.

Logan swatted his head. "Watch it."

Garrick pulled over at the next gas station.

Another forty minutes and I had eaten all my snacks. "This is SO damn boring," I complained.

Logan was worried. I tapped into it, exploring why. He had been paying attention to our surroundings, which were increasingly rural. So rural we had transitioned to a dirt road.

"Park here," Blake instructed.

"The old ones always did love their caves," Garrick complained, adjusting his expensive suit.

We piled out and I sent out my awareness, finding the same natural and powerful magic as The Oracle's. I turned, seeing only thick, lush trees, towering mountains with thick patches of snow, and a blue sky.

We were silent, eyes alert and scanning, as we followed Blake down a trail heavily wrought with rocks and overgrown tree limbs, finally emerging at the mouth of a cave. It was dark and I couldn't see a damn thing. I was probably the only one with that problem.

Logan moved behind me, staying close to guide me. Dread moved into my stomach, and the purity of the darkness was unnerving, my breathing escalating. Down, it felt like we were slowly moving down, the air stagnant and overpoweringly humid.

I ground my teeth, trying to steady my nerves. Ahead, a pinpoint of light appeared. We turned a corner and entered a large cavern illuminated by torchlight.

"How medieval," I muttered. Let's add the cloaks that the four Vampire Council members were wearing along with heavy, gaudy jewelry, and I figured we could get our own HBO show.

The Vampire Council looked down upon me in their dank cave.

"You killed Tate," Eduardo said.

"Yep," I answered.

"You killed Zachariah," he continued.

"Yep," I repeated.

"You left hundreds of vampires Masterless," Eduardo continued on.

I stopped answering him, because technically he wasn't asking questions. He didn't find it amusing, sneering at me, one side of his lip drawing up to reveal his fangs.

I smiled.

Stop poking the hornets' nest, Logan sent to me.

Make me, I responded.

He grunted, shifting his hands in his jeans pockets. Technically, Logan had killed both of the Master Vampires, but believe me, if he hadn't, I would have. Tate had joined Houses with Zachariah; granted, Zachariah had starved Tate's House, but Tate had known of his plans to kidnap my unconscious ass from the hospital.

That just wasn't cool.

Zachariah, his list of transgressions was too long to recite, but I'll give it a shot. Kidnapping and torturing Logan, funding shifter experimentation with Sage, not to mention Nari, and releasing eighty rogues loose on the city, killing hundreds of humans.

We had done what we could, protected our house and as many humans as possible, but even we lost. Grams's memory blasted across my mind and I felt the pain all over again. Even though we hadn't been on speaking terms, her death, well, it sucked.

I blinked, feeling Logan's answering emotions along the mate bond as he warmed me with his love, his annoyance taking a back burner.

"Give us one reason not to destroy you and your pathetic Council," the woman next to Eduardo commanded.

I laughed. "You really want to reconsider that statement," I told her.

"You will show us respect!" she hissed at me.

I groaned. "Look, you archaic excuse for a Council, you fucked up. Whether you knew of Zachariah's plans or not, shit didn't work out for you. The Council and the Shifter Nation are united. The humans are terrified of vampires now after seeing the horror the rogues unleashed, so I feel confident they'll come over to my side. I'm not scared of you. I'm not intimidated by you. I am however, exceptionally annoyed, and I want my bill paid for cleaning up your fucking mess!"

The four them just stared at me. I'll admit it, I stomped my foot. I'm pretty greedy, and I expect to get paid when I clean up other's messes.

All their eyes glowed amber. I chuckled, good, they were pissed off. So was I.

"You will fall," Eduardo threatened me. Logan growled next to me.

"Say it again," Logan hissed.

Eduardo looked at me, not blinking, not moving, probably trying to judge just how fucking crazy we were.

"Let it go. Own your mistakes and move on," I told him, shaking my head. I had no use for this or him. "I have shit to do."

Garrick and Declan had been silent in the exchange, until now.

"If that is all, we will be taking our leave," Garrick said, turning to leave.

I was still staring daggers at the Council, seriously questioning the consequences of killing them all.

"No," whispered Declan. My head whipped over to see Angelina holding a silver blade in Garrick's heart.

The moment dragged out, her deranged and unhinged smile, the cracked teeth. She pulled the blade from Garrick's chest with a sucking sound.

Declan tossed magic, restraining her, and we both rushed to Garrick, catching him as he fell into my lap. Declan shoved his hand into the wound and I felt the raw outpouring of magic flowing through him. With hardly a thought,

I placed my hand on his wrist, pushing up his suit sleeve, the blood staining the pristine white.

"Take what you need," I whispered to his surprised gaze. He didn't hesitate, pulling instantly, deeply. I felt the vertigo and closed my eyes for a long moment before looking down at Garrick.

Which I had been trying not to do.

"Don't leave me," I whispered, my right hand cupping his face. His dark eyes were clearer than I had ever seen them.

"All beings die, Olivia," he said with a small smile.

"No, you aren't going to die," I whispered, bending down to kiss his forehead. "Please, Garrick," I begged.

He reached a bloody hand to touch my cheek. "It has been an honor to fight alongside you. You have grown into an incredibly powerful, beautiful woman." He coughed, "Always trust those powerful instincts, Olie. I love you."

He reached down and pulled out Declan's hand. "Do well, apprentice, the Western Council is now yours. I have lived a good life."

Dust. I was holding dust, and it spread over my legs. Into my lungs I sucked it, my mind trying to reconcile what had just happened. Garrick had been my first ally. The first one who acknowledged my power and status. The first one who had believed in me and my Council. He had been a listening ear and a source of help on so many occasions.

Now he was gone, slipping through my fingers. This was all my fault.

"No, no, NO!" I screamed, fisting the dust, feeling it slip between my fingers.

"We were guaranteed safety," Logan said softly.

"Angelina escaped from our dungeon. You have our deepest sympathies." I turned to see Eduardo smiling.

"You bastard," I whispered.

Declan was silent, except for the bunching of his jaw muscles. I watched him closely before turning to Logan.

"He is yours to avenge, Declan," Logan whispered.

"You can do nothing," the weasel stated. "We kept our bargain, we can hardly be responsible for a crazed woman escaping and attacking you. Especially since you made her Houseless."

"Incorrect," Declan said, steadily standing. I hesitated, looking back to the pile of dust that had been Garrick. "You granted us safe passage. We require a death for a death."

Eduardo sneered. "He trained you well. We will convene on it and get back to you."

"No, you won't." I said, standing next to Declan.

"Then I suppose you won't be leaving," Eduardo said. I felt his fear rising, along with Declan's power. It was impressive. I had been pretty sure he was holding back earlier.

"We claim you, Eduardo," Declan said. He shed his glamour and I stood in awe of him. Shirtless in worn leather pants, his right eye white with only the faintest impression of a pupil and iris, a thick scar beginning on his forehead and continuing past his cheekbone, he stood as tall and almost as broad as Logan.

I whistled, admiring his brown hair, long and decorated with beads and feathers.

His hands moved and Eduardo looked terrified. Good, I thought. He should be.

"Let this be your warning, Vampire Council," I said softly.

With a flourish of fire, Eduardo went up in smoke, screaming the entire way.

I tried to blame the misting in my eyes on the smoke, but my heart hurt. First Grams and now Garrick. Logan's arm went around my shoulders as we left, the Council behind us screaming for our heads, none daring to make good on those threats.

Garrick's body had turned to dust, forever to reside in the dark tunnels. That felt wrong on so many levels, but what could be done?

"Angelina," I said softly, stopping.

Declan snapped his fingers and I heard her screaming as the scent of burnt hair drifted up to us.

I stopped, wondering if it was enough. "Come, Olie," Logan whispered at my shoulder.

"Should we just leave? Should we kill the rest of them?" I asked Logan and Declan.

"It's taken care of." Logan ran a soothing hand over my shoulder and down my arm, taking my hand. I nodded, trusting him completely.

We exited the cave and I blinked, adjusting my eyes. Logan stopped, turning to the dense foliage. It took my eyes a moment to focus on the hulking chocolate bear hiding in the shrubbery.

"Holy geez," I muttered, taking a step back.

The bear huffed and I looked at Logan. "No way," I muttered.

Logan smiled. "Yes, that's Bear. Since he's the Western Compass Alpha, I called for him."

I nodded. "To do what?" I asked.

"To be sure they understand exactly who is in charge here."

I smiled and nodded. "Hey Bear," I called out, my voice dripping with sadness. I heaved a breath, turning away, not having it in me to tease him as I normally would.

...

Logan drove away from the caves, his phone GPS chirping out directions, although for the moment it was only saying "head south" repeatedly. He scowled at the device, needing to take his anger out on something. Looking in the rearview mirror, he tuned into Oliva's emotions; she was shocked, horrified, and blaming herself, as she always did.

"Where do we start?" Olie asked, more of herself than of anyone else, her eyes unfocused.

Declan's face was drawn, his real face. He hadn't bothered to re-glamour or whatever precisely his trick was.

"We need to know who is supplying them with power, how they tracked me, why..." Her voice trailed off. "...Why would they kill Garrick?" she whispered.

"He saved us," Declan stated.

"What?" Olie asked, leaning toward him, elbows resting on her knees. She tilted her head to the side, her hair spilling over her right shoulder.

Declan turned to her. "We could have saved him, Olie. We could have healed his heart, repaired the damage and brought him back from death. But we would have used all of our magic, all of our power, and been worthless after." Declan turned to look at Logan in the rearview mirror. "I'm certain they had more vampires at hand, more than enough to handle both of you as well."

156

"They wouldn't have dared," Olie whispered.

Logan shifted his attention back to the road as he turned onto pavement. Silence filled the back of the car.

...

Declan was hurting. Loss, betrayal, and just as much blame as dominated my heart were overwhelming his. I reached out for his large hands. He didn't grate on my nerves in this form.

He looked over at me, one green eye and one white searching my face.

"Let me help," I whispered softly.

He looked at my hands, and to his own, both crusted with Garrick's blood. It broke my heart. He reached out with rough fingertips, brushing over my palm before intertwining out fingers.

I just held on to him for a moment, analyzing and absorbing. I sectioned off his grief, pain and self-blame, wishing I could do the same with my own, and pulled. His head tilted back, an inhale of surprise on his lips. I coiled the raw and volatile emotions down deep, storing them as I always had, but knowing I could draw upon them now in a way that killed Fae.

I closed my eyes, seeing only our magic, only our power. I sectioned off the blame again, merging it with my own and releasing it. I let it go, it was too heavy to keep, too weighted.

I opened my eyes to find Declan's arms around me.

"Thank you," he whispered into my ear.

I nodded, pulling back, needing Logan. His touch would soothe.

"I need to make a few phone calls ... to ... to make, to make arrangements..." Declan's voice trailed off.

I nodded, slipping into the passenger seat next to Logan. He reached out to grip the back of my neck. I leaned into his strength for just a moment. I wanted to fall into him and fall apart, but I didn't. I couldn't. We still had a Fae Queen and a Succubus Queen on the loose.

"Call Tommy," I asked of Logan. He hit a button the on steering wheel, issuing the voice command. I didn't even bother trying to listen to him. I was slowly condensing Declan's and my own emotions, until I would be left with nothing, yet again.

You will always have me, Logan silently whispered, taking my hand and kissing my knuckles.

My sigh was broken. I did. I had love.

"Hey, boss," Tommy said over the car speakers. Logan adjusted something to limit the volume just to the front seats.

"Tommy," I said, blinking back my tears.

"What's wrong?" he asked.

"Garrick's dead," Logan said, and I squeezed his hand, silently thanking him.

"Blake was able to track me. I need to know how."

Tommy was silent for a few moments.

"When was the last time you saw them in St. Ann?" he asked.

I turned to Logan. "At Eduardo's?" I said.

Logan nodded. "You had your phone on you?" Tommy asked.

I shrugged, "Probably."

"Toss it," Tommy instructed.

I didn't even hesitate. I pulled it from my pocket and threw it out the window.

"Logan, you too. Get to town and get burner phones. I'll see what I can dig up."

"Understood." Logan tossed his phone as well and ended the call.

"Your phones?" Declan questioned. "That's how he tracked you?"

"It's our best guess. We didn't even know where we were going until we got there," I said with a sigh.

I rubbed my temples, the pieces not fitting together. "That doesn't explain how they got to the caves, though. If we didn't know we were coming here, how did they?"

"And how did Luharposn know where we would be?" Declan asked.

I sighed, looking at Logan. "There's a mole in the Western Council."

...

Declan denied our accusations vehemently. I was too tired to fight with him, waiting outside the phone store while Logan took care of the details.

"Impossible," he said again.

"I'm not arguing this point anymore," I told him. "We need to get back in contact with my house for updates. We still have the Queens to find."

Declan sighed, "They must be here."

"I'm open to ideas on finding them."

"Enough," Logan said, jerking our attention to him with a slam of the door.

"Let's go," I muttered at Declan.

...

Logan watched Olie and Declan, still fighting over the damn mole at the high-end hotel Declan insisted they book. He was grateful Olie had relented about accommodations. He hated the flea-infested motels she preferred.

He had already texted Tommy and Becky to have them hack Garrick's information structure.

He tuned into Olie's emotions again. She was worn, and needing something to kill or fuck. He was fully hoping it was the latter.

"So you can track her with my blood?" Olie asked Declan.

"I can," he responded, relief easing over both of their faces.

"Great, when can we start?" She was excited and pushing ahead without thinking through what she was doing. What else could he expect?

...

"Wait, what are you two planning?" Logan asked.

"We can use my blood to find the Succubus Queen."

"I'll need—" Declan began.

"You only need blood?" Logan interrupted.

"Yes, and some other magic," Declan continued.

"Will this hurt her?"

"No, Logan, I'll be fine."

"I didn't ask you, Olie, you will do anything to see this done with. Including taking insane risks," Logan reprimanded me.

I didn't have anything to say, since he was right. Seriously annoying trait.

"It shouldn't harm her," Declan said. Great, now Logan was REALLY was going to be right.

I sighed, leaning back against the headboard, waiting for Declan to expand upon the risks associated with tracking down my mother.

"Because the connection to the Queen isn't strong, it may take a great deal of blood," Declan admitted.

"See? No biggie," I tried to minimize it to Logan.

"Olivia, do you not remember when you drained yourself in order to hunt down the puppet master?"

159

"Of course I do! How could I forget all the bonding we did?" I said with a smile.

Okay, so it wasn't so much bonding as being in a half-drunk stupor from being exceptionally low on blood so I could track Logan's grandfather in his undead state. That's when I had first used my power, to strip control from the sleazy Steven and free Lawrence. If only I had known then what I knew now.

Logan smiled fondly at me.

Had the hots for me even then, huh? I teased him.

His smile widened.

"I knew it."

"Like you didn't have them, too," he answered, pulling me onto his lap.

I leaned against him, my hands slipping under the back of his shirt to the warm skin I needed.

I'll always love you, I sent him, surprising myself.

Stop it, we will see this through.

Logan, the eternal optimist. But as Garrick had said, all things die.

Chapter 14

And so we were back in the woods. The pedestal had more decorations this time, but the main one was me, bleeding into a copper chalice.

"This brings back memories," I groaned.

"The witches," Logan said, watching my crimson blood pool and drip off my wrist.

"Yeah, they were a fun bunch," I commiserated with him.

"That's enough to start," Declan said at my side, handing me a bandage. I wrapped up my wrist, turning to Logan. He slung an arm around my shoulder while we watched Declan work.

"Do you need another map?" I wondered, stifling a yawn. Darkness had fallen and it had been a long day. I was done.

Declan didn't answer, so I shrugged. Logan's head tilted, looking out over his shoulder and away from me. I waited a moment, expecting him to turn back to Declan's chanting. After another moment, I leaned forward, looking around his massive shoulders.

"What the fuck?" I whispered. "Do you think Declan is doing that?"

"I hope so," he replied.

Yeah, me fucking too. The growing darkness was a perfect circle, perfectly black, sucking the light in and spinning. My arm tightened around Logan. I was curious to probe the circle with my magic, but not crazy—well, not at that moment.

We both looked back to Declan, his eyes open as he manipulated the portal with his words, fierce determination etched on his face.

Our rest in the hotel room had been brief, no one much in the mood for sleeping. Declan still hadn't changed back forms and I had to admit, I liked the non-glamour side of him better.

I wanted this done. I wanted to find the Fae Queen, find my mother, and be done with all of it.

The ground shook beneath our feet, and our gaze swung away from the portal of black to a portal of white on the other side.

"Shit, that's not us, is it?" I asked.

The portals jumped at each other, tendrils of power, with us caught in the crossfire. Logan was ripped from my side. "No!" I yelled, my voice lost to the abyss around us. I couldn't see, a perfect darkness rendering my eyes useless.

"Daughter," I heard whispered.

I tried to turn to find the voice of my mother. Flopping like a fish, my body tumbling head over feet, I didn't know which way was up or down, or where the voice was coming from.

"Daughter," it came again, stronger.

I abandoned the idea of trying to move with my limbs and merged into my second sight. Logan was there with me. I wrapped my energy around him, drawing him near.

Nothing happened.

Dammit.

I tried again, reinforcing the previously thin strands into thick cords.

Again, nothing.

Blowing out a breath, I reached out again, but instead of drawing him near, I tried pulling myself closer.

I moved, but had no voice for celebration. Logan's arms reached out to anchor me to him. I searched for Declan next, reaching to the outer level of the darkness. It snapped, and a blinding light followed.

I sucked in my first deep breath, turning to find Logan at my side, both us sprawled on the desert sand.

"We are in Fae," Declan commented.

"I hate this place."

"You shouldn't now, our magic will be more potent, more powerful here."

I should have taken comfort in that. But the memories of being here and of Luharposn were threatening to give me a damn panic attack.

I looked around the stark desert landscape, grateful at least that the sun wasn't blistering hot. Turning, I saw the grouping of trees in the far distance and growled. This was it, the memory, down to the perfect details.

"What's wrong, Olivia?" Declan asked.

"Someone is playing with me," I growled, and began walking. Just as before, the ground moved too quickly and we arrived at the impossibly tall trees in moments.

"Whoa," Logan muttered.

"Stay close," I told him. Was shifting magic? Would he be able to do it here? Was he just as defenseless as I once was? I would have asked Declan, if I thought it was safe to do so. He seemed to be veritable family with the Fae's world.

Either way, we were all staying close.

The trees bent above our heads, forming a tunnel, and I heard my mother's scream. Instinctually, I quickened my pace, even though she was the heartless bitch who had sold me as a baby. I suppose some instincts are just hard wired.

The tunnel opened into a clearing, tree limbs intertwining to form a perfect dome. I looked up at the massive space before my gaze came to rest on my mother, chained to bed, heavily pregnant.

"Daughter!" she cried out, reaching for me, one hand against her swollen middle.

"What the fuck?" I whispered.

"You must help me!" she screamed.

A form moving too quickly for me to track slapped her before coming to stand before me.

"Fae Queen, so glad to see you are back where you belong," I growled.

"Oh, my darling Olivia. I am overjoyed that you have decided to join us." Unlike her sister, with her cold and harsh facial features, this Queen was soft—gentle cheekbones and a button nose, her hair braided up in flowers and ribbons. It was a peaceful face, except for the eyes. Those were just crazy.

"I'm not joining you," I told her.

She shrugged, looking all of thirteen years, except for the towering height. I marveled at her lithe frame, her perfectly unblemished skin.

"No matter, now I can build my army even faster!" With a wave of her hand, several more succubi and incubi appeared, all chained, all looking miserable.

"You've enslaved my race?" I asked, shocked. I might not have liked these people, but they were MY people.

She smiled, a crazy, unhinged, off-her-rocker smile. "They are all mine. They belong to me. My new pets."

"You're insane."

And just like that, crazy bitch snapped, slapping me, wrenching my head around on my shoulders. Logan lashed out claws—well, that was a good sign—slashing though her skin. She screamed, flinging him into the intertwined branches.

"Bitch, that is my man," I grunted at her, shoving her back. She flew backwards, hovering above the ground.

"Where the fuck is Bob when you need him?" I groaned.

"Here, Olie. I am here."

I looked up at the tired jail to see Bob also chained. What the fuck?

I fixed my eyes back on the Queen. "So what, you are delusional and power hungry, going to take over not only your world but ours as well?"

"All of them," she added, her eyes glazed over.

"Great."

"Can I kill her now?" I asked of no one in particular.

"No!" Bob and Declan said.

"Great. Killing would be so much easier."

"She will be hard to kill, anyway, but focus on maiming and injuring," Declan supplied.

"Wait, you aren't helping?" I asked.

"I can't move," he admitted.

I grunted.

"Your magical babies will be superb fighters," the crazy Queen said.

"Bad news bears, I can't have children."

She tilted her head at me like a damn bird, at impossible angles, before snapping her fingers. "There, problem solved."

My insides twisted and I screamed, bending over and clutching my lower abdomen. Logan was at my side as I writhed and kicked, needing some outlet for the intense ripping, searing, and utter agony inside of me.

It was then the bitch chained me. Flopping around, I was vaguely aware of the sound of metal clanking together on my ankle as I fought for control and a clear head. Logan growled, staying close to me, but unable to do much.

Finally, my breathing evened out and the raw agony diminished.

Logan looked down at me with a mix of concern, and dare I say hope? Had she actually repaired what Selena had broken? My hand trembled at the thought of shifter and succubus babies, well let's not forget magician babies as well.

Logan followed my train of thought, reaching down to stroke my cheek. "Let's test that theory later."

I nodded. Right, crazy bitch to deal with.

"Declan, you still pretending to be a statue?" I asked, watching the Fae Queen circle him.

"Unfortunately," he responded uneasily.

I couldn't blame him, I was worried she was going to try and eat him, and not in the good way.

"Bob, you got any helping hints on getting out?" I called.

"No, these chains are impossible. Only—" The Queen turned, waving her hand, her eyes turning red while Bob choked, unable to speak.

"Silence!" she roared. I felt the command against my chest and the large jail she had created fell painfully silent.

"Well, that's a neat trick," I panted, needing to disobey her.

How the fuck was I getting out of here? I certainly wasn't going to try to create a baby with Logan while chained to a bed—well, at least not with an audience.

Logan shook his head, he wasn't restrained. She didn't view him as a threat, but I wasn't testing the theory about Logan having magic here. Wait! I could check. I blinked, trying to pull up my second sight.

Nothing happened.

I tried again. "Shit, these fuckers can block my magic," I groaned to Logan.

He nodded, reaching down slowly to not draw the attention of the crazy bitch. The scent of burning flesh accosted my nose and I moved to him as he pulled away. We both looked down at his hand, not healing.

"You have to be careful," I whispered. He nodded. He'd die for me if I didn't watch him.

I needed the chains off, and now. Turning to Bob, I watched him use a long and apparently sharpened nail to cut long, thin tracks on his arm that dripped blood.

"Did he go crazy?" I whispered to Logan.

Given Bob's exasperated expression, I was missing something.

"Blood, Olie, " Logan mouthed to me, jutting his chin at The Fae Queen.

I groaned, this was going to hurt. "Don't interfere," I warned him.

He took a step back and I took a breath.

"Hey, crazy bitch!" I yelled. Oh gross, did she just lick Declan?

Her eyes still red, she jerked her head to me.

"You dare speak to me?" she hissed.

"Yeah, hooker, I dared."

Quicker than a damn vamp, she had me by the throat. "Not so talkative now, are we?" she preened, grinning manically.

I kicked her in the gut. She learned forward, unprepared for a physical assault. Hoping my nails were long and jagged enough, I raked them across her cheek.

Thin scratches appeared. I looked at my hand, finding that under my nails I had flesh, and a few drops of blood. Now to touch the shackle and hope that for once, Bob was telling the truth.

I dangled there like a fish, swinging my body weight, feeling her grip tighten on my throat. "You are more trouble than your offspring are worth," she seethed.

My vision was darkened. My body not responding to the commands I was giving it, I struggled in earnest against her hold, choking.

I landed hard on the ground, the Queen on top of me. I sucked the beautiful oxygen into my lungs. She turned to face Logan.

His injured hand was at his side, dripping blood.

Dammit.

She was not going after him. I clawed her again, my nails separating flesh, and slapped my bloody fingers against the shackle on my ankle. It clicked open. Tossing it away, I stood, watching her move so damn fast to Logan.

I didn't have a moment to think. Instinct guided my next move, imagining Logan in a protective bubble.

She bounced against it, her hair slowly rising with a life of its own. Guess I had my magic back. I flexed my hands at my sides. It was on.

She turned, fangs descending in her mouth. Well, that was interesting. I suddenly was super curious as to the vampires' creation stories.

"You will not be the one," she hissed at me.

"The one to what?" I asked.

Bob was moaning and bouncing around. "Give me a minute," I muttered, not daring to take my eyes off her. Nor was I lowering the protective bubble around Logan, even with the stink eye he was giving me.

She came at me with the force of a bull and the speed of a damn striking pit viper. I flew back into the intertwined tree branches with a dull thud, before slamming into the ground.

"Ouch," I grunted. Pulling myself to all fours, I looked over at Declan, calling up my second sight and seeing the angry red strands of Fae magic surrounding him.

I pulled from my stores of emotions, the raw pain and devastation at losing Garrick, forcing down a sob as I summoned their power. I infused her magic with it, letting my dark strands overtake hers of blood red.

I turned to look at her stricken face, a hand going to her heart. "What ... what are you?!"

"I'm the fucking Queen," I told her, slamming more speed into turning the braids. I watched as they crumbled, turning into ash.

"That's better," Declan said.

"Did she really lick you?" I asked in a whisper as we moved closer together to take on our common enemy.

"Is that really important?" he asked, exasperated.

"Yeah."

He didn't offer an answer, I didn't expect one. I saw it, she had.

With a roar—that surprised me—she grew in size, coming at us. We didn't stand a chance, blown back into the trees again. Well, at least Declan was free and Logan was protected. I slammed down on a knee and fist.

Play time was over.

Running at her, I used my weight to move her ... like an inch. Fucking hell. Pulling back, I ducked below her fist blow. If she used her speed, I'd be shit out of luck.

I blocked low, my forearms screaming from the assault. I was panting, trying to keep up with her speed. Too bad she was crazy. She would have made an excellent sparring partner.

In frustration, she head butted me and I saw stars, stumbling backwards. Declan chanted, trying something magical.

She laughed, snapping her fingers and suspending him in the air.

"I just got you free!" I yelled at him.

"I'm aware!" he yelled back, trying to use his magic to free himself.

She tackled me from behind, landing blow after blow against the back of my head. I covered the best I could against her assault, but I wasn't doing anything to get her off, either.

"OLIVIA!" Logan screamed.

Nope, not getting out, buddy, I thought to him or maybe myself. Either way, I needed to stop being her punching bag.

I pulled my knees up under me. Pulling my arms from over my head, I slammed my right elbow back into her head. The punching stopped. Turning around, I saw her dazed look and pounced, landing punches into her side and kicks against her knees, annoyed that I couldn't reach her face.

With that damn impressive roar, she picked me up by the back of my jacket, dangling me in front of her massive jaws and razor teeth.

She opened her mouth and I fought harder, no fucking way she was EATING me! Nope, not today, sister.

I reached back, touching her fingers that held me. I had killed this way before, I could do it again. Instead of pushing, I pulled. I consumed the energy I took from her, feeling it fill reserves I didn't know I had, sating a hunger I had grown accustomed to. I took and took and took, until I had depleted her magic and moved on to her lifeforce. Down I pulled the sweet nectar, gorging on the feast.

"Stop, Olivia," Declan whispered.

"Enough!" Logan yelled.

"Kill her, daughter!"

Well, that was enough to jerk me to stopping, even if it was delicious.

I didn't feel my knees hit the ground. I sat back, breathing heavily. With an audible click, the chains released the captives, but no one moved, not even my mother. Declan fell silently and popped the bubble around Logan.

He came to me, arms outstretched. "Are you okay?" he whispered, gathering me close.

I nodded, burying my head in his shoulder, the raw sensation of being magically full new and uncomfortable.

Placing his hand on my cheek, he looked me over. "Your eyes, Olie."

"Black?" I asked.

"Red," Declan said, coming to stand behind Logan, his gaze worried. I closed my eyes and leaned into Logan's warmth.

I felt the Ice Queen's presence along my overworked nerves.

She looked down at her sister's prone form. "She is close to death."

"She's alive," I said. "Now send us home."

...

We landed back in the same clearing where we had started, only with the entire pure bloodlines of succubi and incubi now dumped there with us.

Including my pregnant mother.

"Well, it's about time I was allowed my throne here."

I pointed at her. "You will NOT be getting a throne."

She shrugged. "We will see about that."

"No, we won't. Because you are going to be Dad's responsibility, and if you step out of line ONCE, I will end you!"

"I am your mother!" she said, shocked.

"And I am the daughter you sold into enslavement! The only reason you are still alive is that innocent life inside of you!"

"Selena sought to breed an army from me! You have no idea what that feels like!"

"You are right! Because no one could breed anything from me, since I WAS that army!"

She had nothing to say to that, so I turned, looking at everyone else.

"Let's go, I gotta figure out how to get everyone somewhere safe. And if you screw with anyone, force anyone to do anything against their will, or in any other way harm humans or Supernaturals, I will kill you quicker than you can blink. Clear?"

"You are letting us stay?" whispered a beautiful female in front with honey eyes.

"Yes. I am."

A cheer went up. "I'm going to regret this," I groaned.

...

Somewhere during the long trip home, my phone beeped at me. Checking the message, I swiped the screen aggressively when I saw Raphael's name.

All is well. I have taken Eduardo's position on the Council and will guide the vampires back to their moral compass. Mal says 'hi.'

Fucker. I wondered if he knew how similar a vamp's idea of "well" was to mine of "fucked up as all hell."

Chapter 15

The succubi and incubi spread out across the country. Some stayed close to us in St. Ann, others went back to Oregon or elsewhere. I didn't care, they knew the rules. So far, no one had made it onto my radar.

Declan looked over the unicorn settlement. "Amazing. I can't believe they are back."

"I can't believe they are real," I said with a laugh.

Tommy giggled, riding one of the mares, too fast in my opinion.

I shifted Ginny on my hip. "Be careful!" I called down.

"I'm fine, Olie!" he yelled back.

Logan laughed quietly. "The unicorns wouldn't put him in danger."

"They better not," I agreed.

I cast a look over at Jerry and Mark, reclining on a picnic blanket where Genevieve wriggled, her little fists swinging around.

I caught Logan's gaze and nodded to them. "Keep an eye on Tommy," I warned.

"He's fine, Olie."

I grunted. I'd take it out of his hide if that wasn't true.

Ginny was only too happy to squirm out of my arms and crawl over to Genevieve.

"Will you take it easy," I told her, sitting her down and calming her mimic of Genevieve's swinging hands.

Jerry laughed, lying on his side next to Genevieve. "It's her playmate," he said.

I yawned and nodded, "True." Katie had taken over watching both the girls, for a raise.

Hearing approaching hooves, I looked up to see Harrison on a unicorn with Kass, and Hannah with Darren. I couldn't help but smile at their exuberant expressions.

A bolt of magic flashed over our heads. Without thinking, I threw up a bubble protecting our babies before turning my confused stare to Anna.

She winced. "Sorry!" she yelled across the distance

"What the hell, Dad!" I screamed at him. "Do not make me come back there!"

His head jerked, neither of us used to me calling him that. I turned around before I could give my decision more thought.

A familiar curse had me smiling. "God damnit, Mindy, you will be careful! Don't follow Tommy!" Mercer yelled, exasperated. I laughed.

It all seemed so normal, so peaceful, and I just wanted to hold onto it forever.

"So you will come?" Declan asked, coming to sit next to me.

I sighed. "Is it really needed?" I responded.

"Yes."

"We will be there," Logan said from behind me as he picked up Ginny, who was lovingly smacking Genevieve's stomach. "We need to put Garrick to rest, Olie."

"I'm not sure I can handle another damn funeral."

A unicorn came up behind Logan, nuzzling Ginny. She laughed, batting at it with her baby fists.

I smiled up at her in Logan's loving arms. We once again had saved the world. Although some Fae like Bob were here, they, too, had stayed off my radar. And trust me, I was watching hard with my double sight. Maybe we could all get along on this little blue and green ball.

Logan kissed my temple. He was insistent that my smell had changed and I was fertile. I told him we would see. No sense in getting either of our hopes up, and besides, one baby in diapers seemed like enough for now.

For now.

For now, our wounds had healed. Our family was protected and growing, and I couldn't ask for more.

Note from the Author

Hey y'all! Well, I certainly hope you have enjoyed the FINAL book of The Succubus Executioner Series. Don't cry! I have another series planned where we will see glimpses of Logan and Olie's life, but for now, they deserve their much fought for happily ever after.

I wanted to say THANK YOU! From the bottom of my heart, this crazy dream of converting my day dreams to actual novels, wouldn't be possible without you! For those of you who have struggled with me while I was finding my voice and an editor, you deserve an extra special thank you. I know those early versions were brutal.

Connect with me!

I love connecting with readers! Please feel free to connect to me on your platform of choice. Review are so wonderfully helpful, if you have the time.

I'm always looking for beta readers who get access to the raw final draft to help me iron our kinks and give their opinion on the story line. Please email me at kimbair@proton.me to be added to the list!

Thank you and happy reading!!

MORE BOOKS by Kim Bair:

Dead Shifter Walking, The Succubus Executioner Book 1

Demigod Down, The Succubus Executioner Book 2

A Witch's Fury, The Succubus Executioner Book 3

A Council of Betrayal, The Succubus Executioner Book 4

Death of a Succubus, The Succubus Executioner Book 5

Legacy of the Succubus, The Succubus Executioner Book 6

Creation of the Dual Shifter, The Dual Shifter Executioner

The Mel Files

Andy's Origin, The Andromalius Chronicles